Wolf

THE HALLOWEEN BOYS BOOK THREE

KAT BLACKTHORNE

Author's Note

Dear Wolf Pack,

Wolves hold a special significance for me, however, I was never a werewolf girlie until I met Wolfgang Jack. This beastly man found me in long lost Celtic tales, European folklore, and hours of research into everything from Little Red Riding Hood's origins to the social dynamics of wolf packs in the wild. Beware, there's breeding with no pregnancy, chasing, and insights into parenthood from a lens I don't think most will expect. Please see the full list of content warnings on my site. I'm honored to be a part of the ancient tradition of spinning Little Red Riding Hood into my own story. One that celebrates women, the best of men, and weaves in dark fairy tales in a way that I hope you enjoy.

Let's howl at the moon together.

Xoxo,

Kat

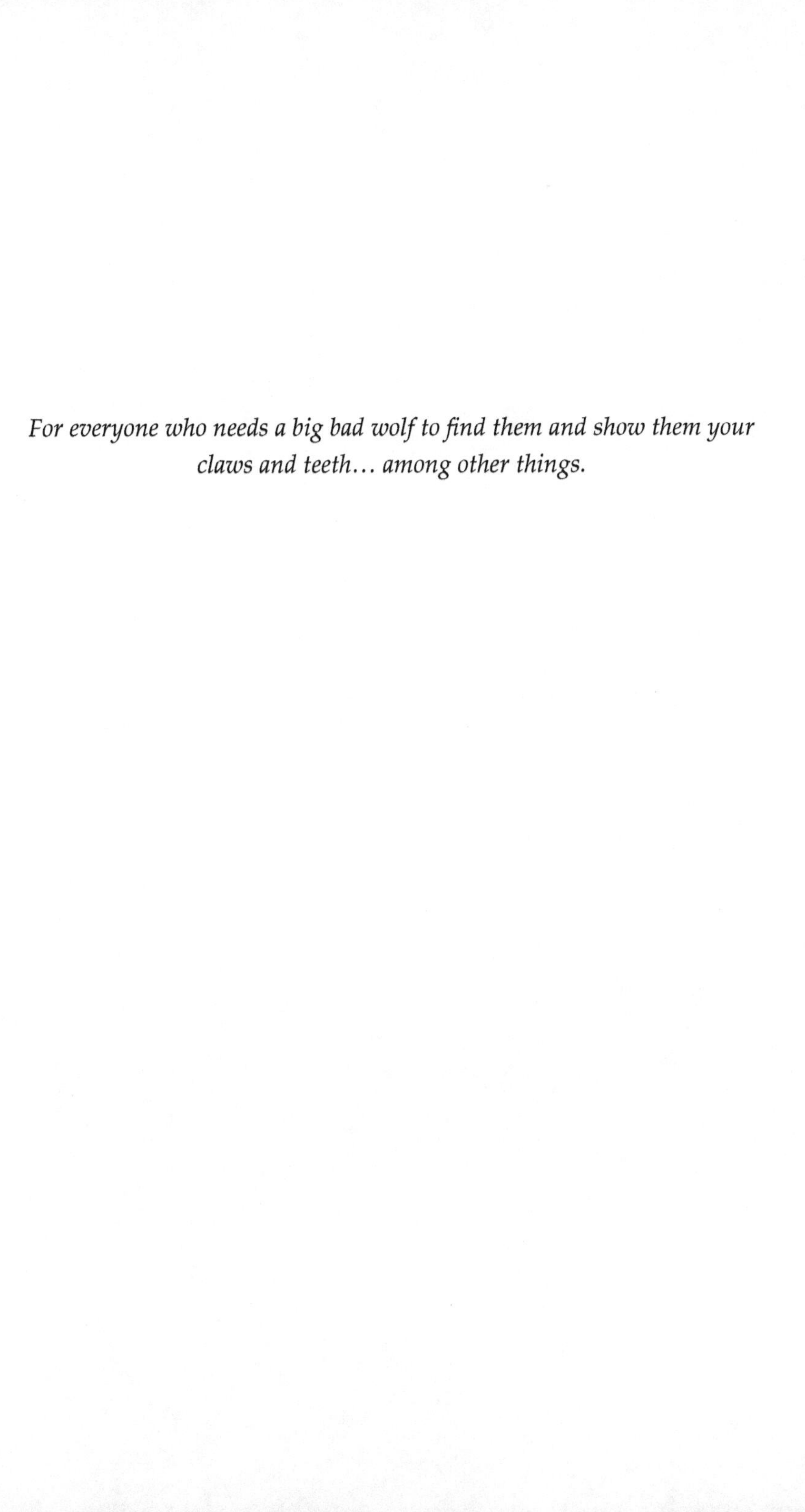

For everyone who needs a big bad wolf to find them and show them your claws and teeth… among other things.

Vibes

Wolf's Playlist

Wolf's Book Board

Pecan Bar Recipe

2/3 cup brown sugar

1/3 cup flour

1 teaspoon salt

1 1/2 cups dark corn syrup

4 large eggs from Fenrir's coop

2 teaspoons vanilla extract

1 1/2 cups chopped pecans (let the pups help but make 'em wash their paws)

1 Heat oven to 350°F or close enough over a fire.
2 Make a pie crust, you know how to do that
3 Bake it crispy
4 Meanwhile, make everything else and put it in the crust. If it smells and tastes good here you're on the right track. If not, eat it anyway, we don't waste food in Fenrir.
5 Bake until all the wolves are beating down your door because they followed the smell from the woods. Cut into bars. No storage instructions because there won't be any left to save.

Oh, and I love you. You're going to be great. Whatever you are, I know it'll be good, Wolfgang Jack.

Love,
Grandfather Jack

CHAPTER 1

Wolf

ONCE UPON A TIME

> So I am still and I am silent, because if I open my
> mouth, I may never stop screaming.
> *Franz Kafka*

I wanted to eat her. The desire to lock my maw around her neck and squeeze as I found her wanting center was overwhelming. The bittersweet aroma of her arousal had been a dull ache in the back of my head for months. But no longer. Not now that I'd felt her walls tense around me, the knot at my base locking us together after our blissful release. There were moments I felt as if it was only the two of us. Not that I minded Ghost and Dragon having a piece of my first complete encounter with her. Perhaps they were all wrong. The Halloween Boys, Onyx's teasing, my pack's skeptical and waiting glances. They all assumed I was an alpha. For Blythe's sake, I hoped not.

I'd waited for her.

Ghost had broken the rules and claimed her first. Dragon had stolen her away and had drunk her blood. I was the patient, supportive friend. They needed my levelheadedness amidst the chaos of their urges. Patience had been instilled in me when I was a pup. The lunas of Fenrir had led us with expert wisdom and precision.

They looked at me as if I'd be their first male alpha, the first sol, in a century. Unlike most, I didn't shirk my responsibility. If it was what my pack needed, I would rise to the challenge. There was only one problem with being an alpha sol, though. When an alpha sol smelled his mate in her rawest form? Well, the legends of werewolves were true. We became slaves to our desire to breed. My body as a man was great, and my wolf form was perfect. But to become an alpha sol would be to let the moon shift me into something that merged both man and wolf.

When the moon was at its highest and when women ovulated, their fertility at its peak... I didn't want to be that monster, that sex-hungry, degrading, half man, half animal that hungered to bed her and impregnate her. It was barbaric and disgusting. She would never look at me as the warm, gentle giant she'd come to see me as.

She'd be afraid, and she would run. She would run, and I would chase her. I would chase her, and I would catch her. I would catch her, and I would fuck her until my seed pooled inside her. I'd knot and keep it there, not letting one drop escape, ensuring she held it all inside. God, something in me wanted her to run. My inner alpha agreed. I'd waited for her long enough.

And it was spring. Blessed Laverna, a wolf's time to celebrate fertility and all it means to be a wolf. The last thing I remembered was our time together in the cold and dead city of Belladonia. We'd gone through a blood ritual, the four of us, but something had happened. I didn't smell Ames or Onyx. I didn't even smell Fenrir. The only scent impression that clawed at my awareness was Blythe and the slickness between her thighs. We were somehow back in the cemetery in Ash Grove. It was now spring, and Blythe was all mine.

When I watched her through the trees, she feared my shadow wolf form and tried to flee. That only encouraged the beast inside me. My little bunny was trying to hop away. How sweet. How innocently tempting. For the first time, I understood why fear turned Ghost on.

Before I knew what was happening, a howl tore through my throat. Informing my pack that I'd found my mate, informing the forest, the trees, the budding earth, and that bright and terrible full moon. I only meant to pounce on her, to cover her body with my wolf. Then it all went wrong. Something happened that never should have, something that had never happened before. When I looked down at my paws, they were the same size, but they were the shape of a man's, covered in fur and long black claws. Blythe screamed beneath me, and I felt my wolf body shift, taking the form of a man but with the likeness of a wolf.

The werewolf, the alpha, the crazed one.

Her body trembled beneath me. I smelled her fear and desire marry in that delectable way that addicted demons, tamed dragons, and entranced vampires. The scent of her sex burrowed into my chest like a fox in its den as a howl tore through me. She screamed, truly afraid then, and I wasn't sure why. And then I realized something I'd always fought against. The thing I never wanted to happen *had* happened. I'd lost control of myself. The kind, gentle Wolfgang evaporated in that moment, and the alpha, Wolf, took control. The territorial, rough animal inside. Her smell had permeated his nose, embedding in his senses, hardening his cock as she wiggled beneath the pads of my clawed hands.

Her neck tensed between my teeth as my tongue lapped up her sweet taste. Wait, her neck was between my teeth? I had her in my grip. Just a touch more pressure, and my fangs would cut the skin and she would bleed. Holding her like that meant she couldn't move. She was helpless and at my mercy. I could do whatever I wanted to her. The beast inside knew he was stronger than the demon, fiercer than the hybrid, and the life to my mate's death. Yes, this was my time. My story of becoming the alpha.

I'd waited long enough.

And I was hungry.

CHAPTER 2

Blythe

FRESH FROM THE BASKET

> I am beginning to despair and can only see two choices: either go mad or turn holy.
> *Adélia Prado*

The Halloween Boys had spoiled me with comfort and safety. Their monstrous proclivities scared me less than the sinister desires of average men. Despite the warnings from others—Ezmerelda's insistence that they were devious, the witch coven's alarm and forbidding skepticism—I'd fallen for them. With Wolf's jaw wrapped around my neck, the truth to the warnings clicked into place, though it should have a long time ago. But I was no better than an average girl ensnared by interest and desire for my villains. No one else could ever compare to the inky release, the blood-stained bliss, and now the jaws and paws of my monsters.

My chest heaved in instinctual panic at the sensation of a wet maw latched around my throat. I wondered if blood from Onyx's bites still stained my skin. Something was wrong with Wolf. He'd never acted this way before, and I was suddenly rethinking everything I thought I knew about the shifter.

When I tried to pull free, his grip only tightened, and a low growl vibrated in his chest. I reached out with trembling hands and found his hard chest. Though he was in the form of a man, a dark layer of fur covered him from limb to limb until meeting the long feet and monstrous paw-like hands of a beast. And his face? The mouth that clamped around my neck was more wolf than human, and his ears lay back as he growled with ferocity as my fingers tangled with coarse fur. I'd only ever seen him as a shadowy black wolf. He'd wrapped me in the shelter of his arms as a human man so many times, but I'd never witnessed this. This was something different and terrifying and new. This was truly a werewolf, and I had the feeling I was his prey.

"Wolfgang," I squeaked a breathy whimper. When I moved, his jaw tightened, so I lay still, pinned beneath his massive, strong form. "You're scaring me. You're hurting me," I whispered, folding my fingers through tufts of fur on his chest. Instead of pushing him away, I pulled him gently closer. His growl turned into something low and seductive, and a ferocious want pulsed between my thighs. Was I attracted to his werewolf form? "I've never seen you like this before," I murmured, straining under his wet clasp around my neck. When he didn't move, I couldn't help but rub the fur along his neck and shoulders, up to his pointed dark ears. Stroking gently, I wondered if it was offensive to pet a werewolf like a dog. But he was very much not a dog. His body was like his, only larger, stronger, with the face of his wolf, his beast.

He seemed to enjoy having his ear scratched, and his jaw loosened. Pulling himself from me, he crouched, still eyeing me like a feral, wild animal. Wolfgang was in there, right? What had happened during our blood ritual, and where were Ghost and Dragon?

I trembled beneath my thin gown in the cool air, and he moved forward. My body startled, and he stopped abruptly, cocking his head to the side to examine my reactions. Running was a bad idea, so I sat frozen, wondering if I was his meal or his lover. Though I was learning that sometimes, with the Halloween Boys, I was both. His large, padded hands with thick black claws wrapped around my arms as he lowered his snout and sniffed my neck. I moved my palm up to cover my bite marks, but he jerked my wrist down, holding me firmly in place as he smelled me.

He sniffed my hair and inhaled along my jaw and collarbone and over my exposed décolletage. Lingering there a moment, he locked his wild amber eyes with mine. Then his focus went back to my throat, only this time, something wet and warm slapped against the exposed skin. The erotic and tickling sensation of him lapping at the sore bite marks left behind by Dragon both excited and terrified me. Pleasure lingered behind the bliss my vampire had inflicted, and my heart constricted, missing him, needing him and Ghost. Had they ever experienced Wolf in this form? I was sure I was doing everything wrong, but at least I'd avoided becoming his meal—for now. Rearing back, he surveyed me again, and as I opened my mouth to speak, the wind was knocked from my chest as he picked me up and flung me over his shoulder.

"Wolf!" I yelled, feeling my body lift high, higher. He had to be the same height as my archdemon when he stood on two legs like this. I beat my fists against his back. "Wolf, this is ridiculous. Would you let me down and talk to me? As a human?" A grunt and sniff were my only response as he stomped through the grave-yard and into the forest beyond. With my ass in the air, I rested on my elbows. "You know, I'm getting really tired of monsters snatching me up at every opportunity. I can walk, Wolf."

But it was no use. Either he didn't understand me, didn't care, or the beast, the werewolf, had completely taken over my friend's functioning. It dawned on me then that I didn't know him all that well. Ghost had captured me, Dragon had stolen me away, and now Wolfgang had become part man, part beast, and I had no clue what was going through his mind. I guessed no one knew except the wolf pack themselves. Oh, that was smart. I leaned up on palms and crawled backward until I was near his pert ears.

"Hey, Wolf. Let's go to Fenrir. What do you think?" His amber gaze flicked to me, and he loosened his grip ever so slightly so I could cradle into his arms. When I wiggled to get down, though, his hold tightened, as if I were a toddler squirming to be let down into a busy street. "Okay, okay. No walking for me," I assured. "But Fenrir sounds nice, right?"

He let out a breath that could have been a yes or a nothing. I guessed I'd wait and see. As I held on to his neck, my newly shifted monster marched me deeper and deeper into the woods.

Into his time, his story, and as a bunny in the mouth of a wolf.

CHAPTER 3

Ghost

THE STORIES WE TELL OURSELVES

> Let everyone sweep in front of his own door, and the whole world will be clean.
>
> *Johann Wolfgang von Goethe*

Beautiful, ethereal, an angel for a demon. Her sighs and watching her wring pleasure from each of us was satisfying and holy. She'd taken to the darkness of demons and monsters, secrets and lies, so nicely. My good little demon whore, my little ghost. My fist was in her hair. It seemed as if hell's smoke surrounded us during the blood ritual. And so why was I not tangled in her afterglow right now? Why was I waking on the other side of bars?

Sitting up, I rubbed my head and looked around in confusion. For a moment, I panicked, thinking it was all a dream. Her, the Halloween Boys, a sick mirage from the sadistic devil that had cursed us. Had he tortured me into hallucinating that an archdemon could find such tenderness in this life? The thought filled me with fury as my haze of delirium subsided, and I beheld black trees dotted with red, and roses—thousands of roses. Perhaps the evil vampire king had planted a rose orchard for his queen. I stood and tugged on the high bars of the gate. Locked. Why the fuck was I in the forest of Belladonia?

Vladimir, Onyx's father, didn't know a lot about demons if he thought a tall wrought-iron gate could keep me out of his cursed city. Within moments, it opened, bendable to my shape. Each strain of my muscles only made me more pissed off. I'd tear apart the framework of the goddamn universe to fix this sick twist of fate that was continually separating me from my Claimed. I'd beat the god of time into submission for pulling this shit. Expanding my senses, I let my hell smoke slither through the vampire town like a tinted blue fog. It could find her quicker than I could, and the boys? Right. Where the fuck were they? The gray castle loomed on the hill overlooking the city, and bats peppered the sky above its storm cloud. My abilities hadn't sensed her yet, or anyone, and I picked up my pace. Hell smoke reached Needle and Thorn and came up short. No signs of life. What the fuck?

In the city, nothing looked amiss. I spotted a few vampires through shop windows as I stalked down the street. If they were anywhere, if they'd left the bar, it would be to go to Onyx's mother. They'd know to wait for me there. As I approached the steps of the gothic castle, I froze. Not much made me freeze in bewilderment, but this did, this sound.

A baby crying.

It had to have been a product of my imagination, an after-effect of whatever black magic had just transpired during the blood ritual. But then I heard a woman sobbing alongside the infant. When I turned, she shuffled out from behind a building, clutching her bundle. Regarding me, she inched forward. "Sir." She sniffled.

I walked up, putting a hand to my chest, finding the woman dressed in old clothing. Old as in from another time, an older time. Trepidation shortened my breaths. "Miss, are you well? Can I help you?"

The woman's puffy eyes flicked from me to the castle, then over her shoulder to the vampire city. Her infant gazed at me with hazel eyes. I sensed them, tasted their fear and confusion on my tongue. They were…

"Where—where am I? How did we get here?"

My smoke rippled like a stone had been thrown in the middle of the town. It sensed what I did, as more bodies appeared, dazed, confused, but not immortal…

Humans in Belladonia.

Humans in the city of vampires.

CHAPTER 4

Blythe

SPEAK WOLF

> That's what artists do, that's what poets do - we all do it. We start with something, and sometimes we destroy everything that we've made in order to get to the core place where we started from.
> *Patti Smith*

He was sniffing—a lot. Sniffing the air, the trees. His ears twitched with every noise, and his eyes were wide and dilated with awareness. It was either a wolf-man thing or something was off. Something felt off, different, and I was feeling as if I was missing limbs without Ghost and Dragon and Raven. I hoped they were here, waiting for us at Fenrir or in the town square of Ash Grove. Each flap of wings or caw of a crow I hoped was my beloved familiar. He'd be where I was. I was sure of it somehow.

Every attempt to be let down from my werewolf's grip proved futile, so did communicating with him. I wasn't even certain he understood me in this form, and it struck me deeper and deeper how little I knew of the wolves. I'd spent some time in Fenrir, but I'd been ignorant in learning these little details, like what to do if your shadow wolf gets stuck in the place between beast and human. My neck ached from Onyx's bites and Wolf's prior grip. These boys were going to kill me if I didn't find a way to take control of my own body, my own abilities. They were older, more experienced at being monsters. I was new, and it was a profound disadvantage.

No, more than a disadvantage. My naivety was a liability, one I needed to rectify somehow. How? Wolfgang's claws tightened on my hip and ribs. He halted his footfalls, sniffing, and his ears laid back. I couldn't speak werewolf, but I knew enough to know that wasn't good.

"What is it?" I whispered, looking around through the woods. Wolf noticed my wandering gaze and huffed a breath and covered my eyes with his large padded hand. "Seriously? I can't even look around?"

Finally, the voice of the werewolf sounded. It was deep and earthy and different. I liked the sound, so different from Ghost and Dragon, though the words were not sweet. "Never gaze into the forest. I smell…" He inhaled and furrowed his brows. "I smell," he repeated plainly.

My heart fluttered in dread and desire, a mix the Halloween Boys had spoon fed me into craving like a rabid frenzy of a wanton creature. Fear and pleasure shouldn't go hand in hand for any normal being, but they did for me, and I liked it. My boys liked it, too. Ghost's taste, Onyx's empathic feel, and now Wolf's sense of smell. What did he smell? Whatever it was, I wasn't even allowed to search for the source.

We continued our trek, though I didn't miss the fact that his steps were lighter, quicker, as night pooled around us, our path lit softly by the full moon. His throat vibrated, a low and lethal sound. Instead of speaking, I held tightly to the fur on his chest, thankful now to be in his arms. When he spoke, the brush silenced around us, as if listening, like he was king of the ground and air and trees.

A smell like rotting flesh infiltrated my nose, making it burn, before I heard my name whispered, and then again and again. Crackled and inhuman, it repeated: "Blythe... we don't see you, but we know he carries you."

Wolf growled, his claws digging into my hips, pricking the skin. I bit my lip to keep from crying out. "My mate's name will be the last on your lips, ghoul. You dare draw near a werewolf in his spring?"

Something heavy moved, followed by another massive being. When I looked over my shoulder, I gasped at the creatures that surrounded us. One was gruesome and as still as stone, as if frozen. If it had eyes, I didn't see them. Only its jagged brown teeth as it sat on its haunches. No, there were three of them... and three more creatures I unfortunately recognized. Their leathery bat ears were tattered and twitching as they exhaled ragged and rough breaths. Four diphylla surrounded us alongside the frozen, gruesome creatures.

"How?" I breathed, tightening my hold on Wolf. Belladonia's shifted, wicked, and transformed remnants of heart-bled vampires were here, in Ash Grove...

"You're going to have to run," Wolf growled lowly. "Run. And do not look back. Do you understand?"

"What? I'm not leaving you—"

Wolf's howl shook the trees, then one beast lunged for his neck, and another moved without being seen as it rammed into his gut. The wind knocked from my lungs as I was thrown against a large mossy oak. Blood sprayed—Wolf's blood—as the monsters descended upon him. But he didn't fight back. Instead, he drew them to him.

"Run!" he boomed, and I could hardly see as tears stained my cheeks. Tears of sorrow and anger at my useless, stupid, non-practiced abilities. I could have helped, I knew it, but the knowledge of how exactly to wield my reaper energy evaded me. Somehow, I pulled myself up and stumbled over the protruding roots, crunching through the fallen leaves, hearing the screams, the high-pitched moans, and sounds of wet smashes withering behind me as I ran like a coward. Like the damsel I didn't want to be, but most certainly was.

MY FEET HURT and my lungs burned, forcing me to slow and catch my breath. I had to be close to Fenrir. I inhaled the bitter smell of smoke in the air and followed the yellow patches of daffodils interspersed between the trees. Wolf hadn't caught up with me, and that filled me with thoughts of the worst. Over half a dozen monsters had attacked him, some of them even from the vampire city, and I'd left him alone. I hadn't had time to myself to gather my thoughts, to process what had happened at the Bleeding Heart Ball. The diphylla died then, but how? I recalled their lifeless bodies as we exited the castle. But I was so focused on the guys, I hadn't stopped to ask questions. But now they were roaming the lands against Fenrir and Ash Grove. The people here were in danger, with no gates, no slayer, nothing to keep them at bay. Where were the wolves?

I'd find them and send them to help. And then I'd find Ames and Onyx. My head spun as I leaned against a tree. Dizzy, thirsty, and with my stomach cramping with hunger, I trudged forward, hoping I was going in the right direction. I passed by purple and orange blossoms, their sweet smell and the sun's rising warmth making me feel lonely and unsure. That probably wasn't the effect flowers had on most people, but I wasn't most people. I was Death. I guessed death and flowers didn't mix. The floral smell became fiercer, and my head dizzied again. I rested on my knees. Could it be pollen giving me an allergic reaction? No, this was stronger, weirder. Around me, the flowers were everywhere. So bright as they whirled, making my eyes droop, begging me to sleep. The patch of green grass I found myself in was so soft as I rested my head, my eyelids unbearably heavy. And then large white paws stopped in front of my nose. Something snarled a wicked sound, and I lost consciousness.

When I awoke, wooden panes were glowing auburn with lantern light. A woman with long white hair leaned against the doorway, her arms crossed as she stared down at me. I made out a faint scar across her eye as she surveyed me, and my mind caught up, still dizzy from whatever had happened in the woods. "Is Wolf here?" I asked, my throat dry. I made to move but found my wrists chained to heavy iron shackles attached to a post in the middle of the room.

"Who?" she questioned, her jaw tense.

"Wolfgang Jack. He lives here in Fenrir."

"Did the circus send you?" she asked, taking a step forward.

"What? No, I'm here with Wolfgang and the Halloween Boys."

"The Halloween Boys are dead."

Panic shot through me. "No," I strained. "Can you please let me go? If Wolf isn't here, he's still in the woods fighting those things."

She kneeled in front of me, resting her elbows on her knees. "How do you have no smell? A new trick of the phantoms?"

An exasperated sigh left my throat. The woman angled her head and reached out, moving my hair off my shoulders. Her arms were rippled with muscle. She was a force, and even knowing nothing about her, I could sense her influence somehow. She rubbed a finger lightly over my tender spots, and my heart ached, missing Onyx. His bites were the only thing remaining to remind me that it was all real, that Belladonia had happened.

"These wounds… so you do come from Vincent. I think it wise not to lie to a luna wolf, invisible one."

"I'm not lying—"

Pain slashed across my face as she struck my cheek. "I wasn't finished talking," she said harshly. "You'll listen. You snuck past our borders, glamored, the phantoms' newest ploy to gain access to our land and our people. It's written all over your used and drank-from body. Though, these"—she fingered freshly sore areas above where Onyx had drunk from me—"these do look as if they came from…" She shook her head. "Another trick."

"It's not," I whispered, fighting to rally my strength.

"Do you know what we wolves do to ghouls? Well, what we used to do, at least. Before… you know. We'd take great delight in torturing them for all eternity. A sacred calling to justice. You've wandered into our den. That's unfortunate for you, because we will torture you as well for threatening our pack."

My irritation and pain and weariness bubbled to the surface then as I fought against my bindings. "Go ahead. I don't mind. Kill me, for all I care. But send someone to check on Wolf, please. I'm begging you. He was surrounded—"

The woman rolled back onto her heels and stood, looking to the side and furrowing her brow. Howls sounded outside the shack, and then her eyes met mine. I could only hope it was him. Then I heard another howl, low and guttural. Nodding softly, I would have felt sympathy toward the luna if she hadn't slapped me.

"Wolf," I breathed.

Several bangs sounded on the door, but as she went to open it, the wood was ripped off its hinges, cracking and shaking the structure. The woman snarled in a flash of white, and in a blink, she was a formidable wolf, her back hunched and massive. But not as big as him, not nearly as big as Wolfgang, who towered over her on two feet. His amber eyes met mine frantically, but instead of softening in relief, they glowed in rage and anger.

And then he went ballistic. The next few moments were a blur of splintered wood and fur, mixed with howls and whimpers as my werewolf tore the structure apart with his clawed hands, throwing wolves off him as they jumped and sank teeth into his arms and legs. He ripped my chains from the ground and picked me up, flinging me over his shoulder again and letting out a howl. This sound, this bellow, was different, sadder, somehow. The activity hushed as fires crackled around us. It was night again, and

I pushed against my sore limbs to turn and see what was happening, why everything had fallen silent.

Wolfgang was coated in blood, his breathing ragged. He didn't fight me when I moved to cradle into his hold and behold the sight of every wolf of Fenrir bowing before him.

CHAPTER 5

Wolf

HUNGRY LIKE A WOLF

Listen to the silence inside the illusion of the world, and you will remember the lesson you forgot.
Jack Kerouac

The foul stench of ghoul and their decay hung heavy in the air, tainting Fenrir, roaring through my blood as I assessed the foreign pack that bent to me, a sign of respect toward this new form. This wasn't my pack. These weren't my lunas. I smelled no elders. My pack would have never allowed grime in the forest of Ash Grove, would have never taken a human-smelling girl to the shed we prepped ghouls for death. A howl tore through my throat again. Anger, disappointment, an intense desire to slaughter them all and start over with only Blythe hounded me. To fill her with my seed, watch her belly swell with my pups, and start our own pack. I could. I could have killed them each then and there. Elders of the past might have for the state I was sensing Fenrir was in. How did these imposters live with themselves?

"You call yourselves wolves? You disgrace this place." I snarled at the white-haired luna on her knees before me. "Where are the elders?"

She met my gaze, then, and dared to slowly rise onto her feet while the other wolves bowed, both in animal and human form. No one looked like me. No one was… what I was now? The white wolf lifted her chin. "There have been no elders for years."

"Where did they go?"

"They left."

Lies. My throat vibrated, and I contested the urge to rip her apart. "Where are the lunas?" The women who led Fenrir would have never let it fall into such a state. But I didn't smell them. I didn't smell anything right. Everything was wrong.

"I am the lead luna here. The other lunas, sols, and stellas, left soon after to find the elders. None returned. There is a sickness in the woods—"

"Sickness you've allowed! You are not wolves. None of you. You're fucking cowardly rodents to me." The temper unleashed, the string broke, and I didn't sense the intensity of my snarl until I felt my mate press against my chest and her heart rate quicken. I was scaring Blythe. Fuck. No, this was all so fucking wrong.

The sorry excuse for a luna looked down and shifted her weight. "It is as you say. We have struggled these years with the attacks and with the lack of protections our full pack afforded us. But now our alpha is here to assist us, as Calliach said he would come."

"One name I recognize, one I do not, one I am not."

"You are," she argued. "You know it. We smell it. Your alpha form is undeniable, or are you the cowardly rodent, Wolfgang Jack?"

Now she sounded like a luna. She stepped forward, and my body lowered, deflated, until I was a man before her, before my pack. My disgraceful fucking wolf pack. I was their scary, inexperienced idiot of an alpha. If I chose to take them on, if I decided to carry Fenrir on my back, with the remaining lunas, through this travesty, how could I right their wrongs while my mating bond and alpha awakening raged inside me? Being an alpha would put me in the ranks of leadership with the lunas, never above them.

Still always in service of them. But with a stronger form and equal decision-making power.

But how could I lead when the moon was turning me into this feral beast that only wanted to mate, to be with my beautiful, delectable Blythe, only wanting to consume her inch by inch? How did this all happen? I'd question the luna later. My mate needed tending first. I marched past the white wolf, parting the sea of wide-eyed boys, women, and pups and heading toward my house. I smelled it, at least. When I arrived at my section of Fenrir, my home had been claimed by moss and grassy gutters. Years. Had we really been gone for so long?

I shook out the dusty furs before gently moving Blythe to lie in them. She hugged her knees while I avoided her gaze, instead busying myself with making her a fire. It was the first of many things she needed, and I'd give her everything I had. Anything to erase her fear of me and prove myself a worthy partner.

"I'm going to find you food and warmer clothing and… bandages." The smell of her blood, of the bruises swelling on her neck, swarmed me like the weight of every failure known to man. I'd hurt her. I'd let this godforsaken pack hurt her. I'd made her run all alone and into poison laverna blooms. Shit.

"Wolf," she whispered. I gritted my teeth before putting another log on the fire. "Look at me, please."

I couldn't deny her when her voice was as tender as a fawn. But when I took her in, my heart broke. Red smoothed into purple around her neck. Cuts were still fresh on her calves. And while Onyx's lingering bite marks were pleasurable and a part of his nature, harming my mate was not a part of mine. *Monster. She trusted you, and at your first opportunity alone with her, you turned into the alpha beast of nightmares. You scared her. You hurt her—*

"Wolf," she whispered again. "You look so sad."

Standing, I cleared my throat. "Don't move. Rest, and I'll be back soon."

Ignoring her objections, I left, but stopped on the porch. My newly unlocked alpha tingled in my blood. I couldn't leave her alone, but I didn't trust any of these asshole Fenrir imposters. And Blythe was prone to choosing the most unsafe option at any given moment.

Looking around, I remembered my bench. Opening the lid, I pulled out my rusty hammer and a stack of two-by-fours. Pocketing a handful of cold nails, I positioned the wood over the door and hammered it shut. Then I added three more boards, sealing it in place. Nothing would be getting in or out. I moved to the window, and Blythe opened the curtain.

"What the actual fuck are you doing?" she screeched, muffled by the glass.

"Keeping my mate safe."

"You're nailing me into your house?" She tried to open the window, but it was no use. I covered it in boards. I'd built too many structures to ever build anything in any manner that wasn't swift, sturdy, and quick. I'd tear them off easily when I returned. My shoulders eased, and I let out an exhale as I pocketed my hammer and marched down the stairs. Blythe screamed like a child behind me, pounding on the wood. But she was a safe child, at least. One that wouldn't be stolen by whatever now haunted the woods or eaten by a wolf. Well, any wolf other than me.

Onyx would be very pleased with himself to see me as the alpha asshole he always taunted that I'd become. Ghost would be concerned for Blythe, as he should be. And Judas… I'd face him when the time came.

As I made my way toward the fires to the pack that at the very least knew to wait for me there, my resounding thoughts were loud and warring. What had become of this place, my people? And where were the Halloween Boys?

CHAPTER 6

Onyx

BLACK HEART

> A very little key will open a very heavy door.
> *Charles Dickens*

My belladonna dripping in red. Tangled in my werewolf and consumed by my demon, as I consumed her taste, her essence, her very existence tied with my two oldest and most steadfast of companions. I'd assumed it was euphoria that rendered me immobile and sent me falling into the dark expanse. But then my head was pounding, beating a thrum of annoying pain as I sat propped on something cold and hard. Decidedly not a bed *or* my luscious woman. My vision adjusted as I sat up and gripped the arms of—the throne? I tipped my head back, taking in the way the seat reached high above my back. Sure enough. The throne.

"I didn't want to upset you with everything going on, but I'm afraid there's something you should see—" The man's familiar voice cut off as the sounds of their clipped footsteps stopped in the entryway.

My mother put her hands to her chest and rushed forward. "Onyx, love. Where have you come from?"

Elysium reached out an awkward arm, as if he wanted to

comfort her, but stopped short of touching her back and thrummed a nervous beat on his chair instead. Clearing his throat, he remembered me. "What is the last thing you remember, Onyx?"

I mean, was I supposed to say the last thing I remembered was being balls deep in my wife, with my two friends, as we all dripped blood and sex? Probably not. Wincing, I stammered, "The uh, bar, your bar, after the Bleeding Heart Ball." I straightened, rubbing the back of my neck. "Is Blythe there?"

"No, my son. We haven't seen any of you for quite some time now. We've been so worried."

"That can't be true," I replied, skimming my tongue over my fangs. Her taste still lingered as if I'd only just bitten her. "Why am I on the throne? Where is my family?"

My mother looked tired, and her blond hair held a more silver tint than before. She looked from Elysium to me, as if hoping he would answer. Her voice rang through my mind. "Something has gone terribly wrong. It would seem you're connected in some way. Come, let's go someplace else. I despise the throne room."

Standing, I wobbled down the dais when the walls shook. Something crashed and the double doors flew open. The second Halloween Boy to storm Vladimir's castle. The thought made me crack a smile of relief, even as Ghost noted the fear on the queen's face and shifted back into his man form. He looked to me and gave me a short once-over, then he turned and regarded Elysium. Pointing, he threatened through gritted teeth, "You."

The slayer held his ground as my friend stomped over and grabbed him by the collar. With speed that took more effort than I wanted to acknowledge, I put myself between them. "Can we cease the tough guy shit and figure out what's going on? Ghost, are Blythe and Wolf with you?" I looked over his shoulder, waiting to see them walk in behind him.

"No, and it's because of him and whatever fucking magic he did during the blood ritual."

"Blythe isn't with you?" Panic seized my throat.

My mother touched my arm gently.

Ames was losing his cool as he pushed Elysium away. "There are women and children out there, right now, crying in these godforsaken streets. Now tell me what the fuck you did and how to fix it and—"

"And how to get our wife back," I finished for him, my own outrage building. I looked to my mother, who only held sorrow behind her expression. Not shock. She'd known about whatever this was.

"The humans are safe," the queen said quietly. "No vampires that remain will touch them. On my orders."

"Send them home," Ames demanded.

Elysium adjusted his ruffled collar, and his chair whirled and clicked as he tapped on a keypad. A holographic image appeared in neon green, displaying the city. There were blue and red dots scattered throughout, flanked by black squares. As if we were supposed to know what any of it meant. "The doors are dead. The magic here has gone haywire. Humans were transported in the middle of their daily activities, and we have yet to find how it happened or the means to send them to their respective homes. It happened the night you all disappeared. For us, that has been five years."

"Five years?" I repeated, meeting my brooding friend's stare. "What the fuck happened during the blood ritual?"

Ames cut in. "He's lying. Whatever he says is a lie. Can't you see? He's vying for the throne, for the queen. He probably orchestrated the entire thing and used us to make it happen. I should kill him where he stands."

Elysium's chair vroomed furiously, as if it was mad all on its own. "That is not what is happening here," he replied sternly. "The ritual should have worked to unite your bonds and restore your home. I do not know what went wrong. Every mate was accounted for during the ritual, correct?"

"Of course," I said hastily, but I noticed Ames's jaw tighten and felt his emotions pool around me like a cold chill.

My mind had sprinted to Blythe and wondered after my

friends while disregarding another player in our game. Another key player. A Halloween Boy who was quiet, elusive, and way too powerful for any of us to dare forget. Though somehow, we often did.

I ran a hand through my hair, hitting something hard. It fell to the ground with a loud, echoing clatter. I kicked the golden crown in frustration, the music of my tantrum bouncing along the stone of the castle floor.

Looking to my demon friend in furious desperation, I lamented, "The Fucking Devil."

CHAPTER 7

Blythe

WHAT DO YOU KNOW ABOUT BARGAINS?

> It's not enough to be nice in life. You've got to have nerve.
>
> *Georgia O'Keeffe*

I was far from an expert on love. I knew that loving someone meant accepting their flaws, their little idiosyncrasies, all their weirdness and oddities. Maybe I expected that to be dirty socks on the floor or left-opened bags of chips. Not, you know, nailing me, board by board, into a house with no escape. And, you know, trying to eat me. Collapsing into a mound of pelts, my body gave out. I could only bang on the doors for so long. Wolfgang was going wild. Onyx had hinted at it, but why hadn't anyone warned me about the magnitude of the insanity? I made a mental note to kick my vampire prince in the shins for not giving me a more thorough heads-up on this half-man, half-wolf thing that was happening. Wolf's stress was evident, and I felt deeply for him. To return to his home and see Fenrir in such disarray?

I guessed I'd be acting pretty unhinged, too. It was especially concerning behavior from him, though. In what I'd seen and experienced from Wolf, he was so stable, steady. A constant source of strength and positivity. And now that our worlds had been upended, could I provide some of that strength to him in return?

I wished Ames and Onyx were here right now. They'd know what to do, how to help him, how to fix whatever was broken in Ash Grove and Fenrir. Ash Grove. Were the diphylla and other monsters attacking people there? My body was exhausted, but my mind wouldn't allow me to rest as the fire slowly sputtered to coals and sticks. The sound of scratching reached me, pulling me to an achy sitting position. What if it was one of the monsters? Pebbles scattered into the fireplace, several at a time, and my heart seized. Something was trying to get in—and I had no way out.

Grabbing the iron stoker, I pressed myself into a corner, my wrists still sore from being bound in chains. This sucked. This constant feeling of helplessness. If it wasn't for Onyx, I would have been bled to death in Belladonia several times over. If it wasn't for Ghost and the willow spirit, I would have been taken by a legion on Halloween. And now, if Wolf hadn't been with me earlier, the new terrors in our woods would have had me in their grasp. I was dependent on them. Death was dependent on her four men. This couldn't continue. I couldn't keep shaking in corners while the guys bore the scars of protecting me. The luna had looked at me with such pity, such disgust. She was strong, a white wolf, a leader. I was weak.

Dirt and soot collapsed into the hearth, muffling out the remaining coals. Coughing, I held out my metal stick, as if it would do anything to protect me. "Stay back," I coughed out, hearing how feeble and stupid I sounded. Death in a world full of fiends, shaking with a stick.

A dark silhouette appeared, ruffling and shifting into something larger than what had entered through the fireplace. As the soot cleared, I rubbed the burning from my eyes, and my heart sank into my shoes.

"I'm here, Blythe." Black winged arms took me into their embrace.

Tugging on his vest, I rested my chin on his shoulder. Relief, sadness, and joy all poured through me. "Raven." I squeezed him tight. "I'm so happy you found me."

He brushed himself off, and I pulled back so his long-beaked mask didn't hit me. His humanoid form always made me smile. "The werewolf is in his spring. Now I see. How lovely. Remarkable creatures, alpha wolves. Though I haven't seen one up close in a very long time." He held my shoulders and looked me up and down, cocking his head in a very birdlike manner. "You look damaged, but I'm happy he hasn't swallowed you whole."

A rough laugh left my chest as Raven picked up a fur and wrapped it around my shoulders before peeling the stoker from my grasp and setting it to the side. I slid down the wall and rested my head on my knees. "Everything's so messed up," I breathed. "I don't know what to do. I'm always at the mercy of monsters."

My familiar was quiet as he sat next to me, putting a kind wing around my back. "You keep forgetting that you're a monster, too."

A sniffle rattled my breath before I'd even realized I was crying. "I don't know how to be a monster. I barely know how to be a human."

Raven ran a long feather along my cheek, drying my tears. "Whatever you are, it's enough. And I'll always be around to remind you of that."

Leaning into his warm, dark, feathery chest, peace finally found me in the arms of my familiar.

A LOUD CRASH and a sudden feral roar startled me awake. Wolf stood before me, chest heaving, sweat sticking his dirty white shirt to his chest. His amber eyes were glowing, and his wavy hair was tied up in a knot. He was angry and holding his head, trying to calm himself. "No one touches you but me or our mates." He growled low and in the sound of the werewolf that lurked beneath his skin.

Dazed, I sat up and looked at my beaked friend. "Wolf, this is Raven, my familiar. Are you kidding me right now?"

Raven stood and showed his palms. "He's in his spring. It's not really him. It's okay." Giving me a wink, he evaporated, shifting back into a bird. He perched on the window frame, cocking his head in interest. Nosy, cheeky bird. Of course he wanted to see whatever happened next.

Wolf let out a steadying breath. "That's better, I guess."

"Wolfgang, what the—"

"Here, I have baskets, lots of baskets of things for you. And this." He kneeled before me, pulling over a bucket filled with milky white water and rose petals. "I'll clean you first."

"Wolfgang."

"And then I'll mend you, clothe you, and feed you."

"Wolf," I pressed, tucking a stray wave behind his ear.

His hand shot to mine, covering my knuckles with his rough and callused palm. "And then"—he nipped softly at my fingertips, fluttering my core with the feel of his teeth—"then, when you're strong enough to take me, I'm going to fuck you. I'm going to fuck you so hard and for so long, Blythe."

Every bit of ache and heat within me pooled between my thighs as my cheeks flushed. Wolfgang bit his lip and gripped the basket so hard it cracked in protest. With a low growl, he warned, "Keep smelling like that and looking at me with those eyes and I won't be able to control myself."

Raven squawked as he leapt over the werewolf's broad shoulders and out the door. "That was enough eavesdropping for Raven." I smiled, picking up the rag from the side of the bucket. "I'll wash off."

With a grunt, he took the rag from my hand. "I said I will be the one bathing you."

"Wolf, what is this? You're different."

"Take off your clothes and I'll tell you."

Remaining on his knees before me, he held my elbows and guided me to stand, knowing my legs were tired. "Should we be worried about the guys? Why aren't they here with us, and how did you and I even get here?"

Wolf only raised an eyebrow and gestured toward my gown, withholding his reply until I gave my cooperation in exchange. I rolled my eyes. "Now you're bargaining like Devil."

"What do you know about Judas and bargains?" he countered quickly; the subtle mirth was gone from his gaze.

Shit. I'd promised to keep my meetings with the cranky old mystery man a secret. In return, he'd help me. And I had a feeling I was really going to need the help of a being as powerful as the devil. Clearing my throat, I pulled off my dirty shift dress. My breasts were heavy and my nipples perked in the cold of the room. The werewolf was immortal, but it didn't matter. Males were males, and his attention was immediately fixated on my naked body.

"Nothing," I replied. "Raven said something once about devils liking bargains, that's all."

Wolfgang hummed low in his throat as he dipped the washcloth into the milky water and inched forward. I braced myself on his shoulder as he started with my ankle, wrapping his hands and the warm, wet rag around it. He moved up in slow, circular movements. My fingers instinctively dug into his shirt. "You talk about my smell, but yours is…" I inhaled. "So nice." Without thinking, I leaned forward, burying my nose in his long hair. Pine and rainstorms and a warm spring day warmed my body as he wet the cloth again and ran it up and down my other leg. When he reached my inner thigh, he looked up, his gaze turning wild as he inched the rag between my soft inner thighs, positioning between them as the water trickled down my knees.

"Your aroma, Blythe," he growled, pushing the cloth over my sex. His face covered the washcloth, pushing a moan from my lips at the feeling of his mouth and nose on the other side of the rough fabric. He rumbled a growl and inhaled deeply. "As good as you taste. Your pussy tastes like honeysuckle in June."

My breathing was heavy as I leaned against him for support.

"We never finished what we started on the boat," I whispered. "Or on our last night in Belladonia."

I wanted him. Wanted to feel his heavy body atop mine. It was selfish to need him with everything falling apart around us, but the state of our world only made me yearn for my protective Wolf even more.

He looked up at me and straightened, pulling away and disregarding my concealed plea. "To answer your earlier question, no. Don't worry about Ghost and Dragon. Wherever they are, they'll find us. I don't know much about magic, but I'm guessing whatever ritual we took part in has something to do with bringing us here. If I had to guess, I'd say it did something similar to them."

"That sounds reasonable to assume," I replied. Embarrassment prickled my skin at his subtle rejection of my advances. Part of me really wanted to coax the wolf man out of hiding and play with him, but he was right. My body in this battered and worn state likely couldn't handle it. I bit my inner lip and let him finish cleaning me. He was so incredibly gentle for such a large, beastly man. I'd witnessed him tear apart structures with his bare hands, the same hands that now ever-so-tenderly plucked a stray rose petal from between my breasts. When he surveyed me, seemingly satisfied, he wrapped me in a clean blanket and motioned for me to sit.

"At least Fenrir still has medicine and food. They aren't complete idiots without the elders."

"Who are these wolves? Do you not recognize any of them?"

He scooped green salve from a jar and began massaging it into the scrapes on my calves. "Some of them smell familiar. Some foreign. The elders are gone, as are the original lunas. Don't think for a moment I trust this pack. I may be an alpha wolf now, but this is not the Fenrir, the home that I know and respect. The state of the woods… I'll figure out what's going on once you're taken care of."

"After you nail me back in here?"

He shrugged. "With snacks this time, though."

I met his slight grin then, and as annoying as he was, it lit my soul. I couldn't help but smile. There was the Wolfgang I knew and loved. "They better be good snacks," I muttered, angling my chin as he worked on my neck.

His long fingers stalled around the line of my throat. "Blythe," he breathed. "I'm so sorry."

The emotion in his tone surprised me. One moment, he was angry, and in the next joking. And now he sounded like he was on the verge of tears. "Why? You've done nothing wrong."

"These bruises on your neck? Marks from my stupid, crazed maw." His jaw tensed, and he lifted my wrists. "These gashes in your palm are from my claws. I did this. I've hurt you; I've betrayed your trust and gone against everything I believe in by harming you."

I cupped his face, my hands so small along his scruffy jaw. "You couldn't do anything to make me distrust you. And Onyx hurts me all the time. He loves it."

Wolf almost smiled but looked down. "You were so afraid. I smelled it, heard your racing heart. You were afraid I would kill you."

"Well, the fear thing is the attribute Ghost loves, so again, I'm not worried."

"I wanted to kill you—devour you is more like it. I could have."

"What?"

"When an alpha werewolf hits his spring, his mating season, taking on his new form for his mate, a sort of frenzy happens under the full moon. All we want is sex, to breed our partner, and we wolves we're... ferocious. Fellow wolves can take it, but you're not a luna. You're so fragile."

For some reason, that hurt my feelings. But he was right; I wasn't a luna. The female wolves were intense and strong and wise. I thought of the white wolf outside, how much better of a match she'd be for him, and jealousy sizzled in my chest.

"But you didn't... devour me. Though that doesn't sound so bad, honestly."

He snorted. "Onyx and Ghost have corrupted you."

"Maybe I corrupted them." I smiled, happy to see him doing the same.

After he slathered me with earthy, gritty ointments, he pulled a shirt over my head and held out loose sweatpants for me to step into. I'd love to see Wolfgang in a pair of gray sweatpants... He insisted he dress me, and I didn't have the energy to argue. Once I was tucked back into his furs, he pulled out several more baskets overflowing with food and a gallon-sized stainless steel tumbler filled to the brim with ice-cold water. After I gulped down nearly half the bottle, I accepted plate after plate of jerky, sausages, carrots, and breads. As I finished, my lightheadedness subsided and my dreary mood lifted slightly. Wolf busied himself spraying down surfaces, dusting, and stocking the pantry with the remaining food before building me another fire. He worked silently, and I watched the way he organized spices and readied every surface for me.

"I forgot flowers for the vase." Disappointment laced his tone as he met my gaze and stoked the fire. "But I loosened all the jar lids so they're easy for you to open. Your hands are so tiny."

I'd never been around a man like Wolfgang, and I couldn't even form the words to express how I felt loved just being in his presence. "Lay with me?" was all I could ask. My full belly roped drowsiness back to the forefront of my body. Though watching the muscles in Wolf's back ripple as he cleaned the countertops was so stimulating I could have woken myself up for him if he'd shown any interest. But aside from what he'd said when he arrived and the brief moment while he cleaned me up, there'd been no interest shown from him. Concern pulled at his mouth as he picked up a piece of wood and nudged it onto the blaze.

"Fire makes me miss Onyx," I said, watching him.

He sighed. "Me too. He'll find us. He always does."

"Are you okay?"

"I will be." He stood and walked over, kneeling again. "Sleep. I'm going to be outside in my wolf form."

"Why? Don't you want to…" I fidgeted with my braid. "I don't know, cuddle?"

The corner of his mouth lifted slightly. "If I stayed in here with you, there wouldn't be any cuddling. And there wouldn't be any sleeping, either. You need to rest. And I—" He rubbed his forehead. "I need to be a wolf tonight and sort some shit out in my head."

Taking my fingers in his, he kissed my knuckles. "I'll be looking after you all night, keeping you safe. Sleep well."

When he left, I tiptoed to the window, finding a crack in the wooden boards he'd mounted. Instead of his large frame and tousled waves, the image of a great, shadowy dark wolf rested in front of the door, ears alert. All I wanted to do was walk outside and sit with him, rub his fur, and give him some level of peace. He seemed sad and disoriented at having returned to find his pack in shambles. I felt deeply for Wolf. He'd made me feel safe and brought a sense of joy into my life from the moment I met him.

He was so different from Ghost, who was pensive and severe. Wolfgang was also the opposite of Onyx, who was an emotional cloudburst of feeling and passion. Could I ever be what an alpha so bright and steady like Wolf needed? Could someone like him even be happy with a being like me? Someone dark and unsure. I guessed I could have gone and asked him. I could have tried a little harder to get him to talk, to open up about how he was feeling. But instead of being brave, I did as I was told. I sank back into my warm pelts and dove into a fitful and cowardly sleep.

CHAPTER 8

Onyx

TIME FLIES

Nikita Gill

My father must have been laughing from his coffin at my predicament. We sat around a long dining room table, discussing the situation at hand. Ames only looked increasingly more annoyed as he listened to Elysium drone on about his theories of what went wrong and how to fix it. Occasionally, my demon friend and I would catch each other's glances and we knew. We both knew we'd fucked up by not consulting our devil, who was a part of our crew and bond, before meddling with magic. Blood sex had sounded so good. Who could blame us? Ames rolled his eyes at me as if he sensed my thoughts.

I shrugged, interrupting the slayer as my mother refilled our wine glasses. "So the humans here are safe, the vampires sated, doors broken, monsters everywhere. That's the gist of it?"

"And apparently, time, at least for you, has been affected as well," my mother remarked.

"If the doors are broken, how do we get home? And where are Blythe and Wolf?" Ames asked through gritted teeth. Poor guy didn't know what to do if he couldn't punch his way out of a situation. He wouldn't survive a day in court.

"Do you know why we appeared where we did? Me on the throne and my grumpy friend here…"

"Outside the city gate." Ames supplied curtly.

Elysium stroked his gray beard, a new addition since the last time I'd seen him. "I would guess with the way I worded the spell. You were all sent to where you belong. An archdemon—I suppose, the farthest the ritual could throw you would be outside the gate where the monsters reside. Onyx, well—"

"Obviously." I smirked, motioning toward my head, where the crown had been.

Ames sneered, "You can be full of yourself after we find our Claimed."

"By that logic, Blythe should be in the diner in Ash Grove. Or somewhere in Ash Grove."

"My church," Ames argued.

"And Wolf in Fenrir, I would guess," I added.

Thunder rumbled through the castle, shaking the taper candles and chandeliers.

A low and chilling voice sounded from the entryway. "Yes, he appears at the opportune moment, just in time to save the day. All eyes on you, Dracul. Bravo, son, just as I would have hoped."

I stood, my chair clattering to the floor. "Who the hell let the bat out of its cage?"

Ames draped an arm over his chair and looked from him to me, raising a curious if not antagonistic eyebrow. We liked to fuck with each other, but I knew he'd kill for me in an instant. I also knew it hadn't escaped his thoughts of how we'd accomplish that. My mother sighed and downed her wine while Elysium crossed his arms. Oh, and there my father was, in all his cliché vampire glory—pale, black hair, and glowing red eyes.

He sauntered closer, picking up a green apple from a bowl and shining it on his velvet coat. "The whole family is together. How delightful. Now, tell us, King Drakon, what's our next course of action?"

My mother looked to me with pleading attention. "I couldn't let him waste away asleep in that wretched coffin forever. It felt wonderful at first, but then I began to feel guilty. He knows he's a servant of the crown, and he has been obedient… mostly."

Elysium snorted, not meeting my father's too-pleased-with-himself expression.

"I'm not the king," I growled. "If I were, I'd kill you here and now. Wait, I suppose I don't need to be the king to do that, do I?"

"You certainly don't," Ames agreed, standing and joining me at my side.

Queen Cassiopeia rose. "No one is slaughtering anyone today, and not in here. I quite like this rug. Besides, the Count knows more about this world, this castle, and magic than anyone. He has helped us in many ways."

"Ah, such a nice guy now. After killing innocent girls, forcing my wife to do your bidding, impaling me in the heart… yeah, I bet he's turned over a new leaf." I crossed my arms, unimpressed. "Clearly, he's taking advantage of your kindness, Mother."

Elysium snorted again, his mouth tight, as if he knew saying anything would earn him a scolding from the woman he so clearly loved. Madness, I loved when Blythe scolded me.

Stepping closer, Vladimir put a hand on the back of my mother's chair. A move that sent Elysium's anger rushing into me like a river of stones. "My son, we must all grow and change. I have done a great many things in my time that are less than favorable in hindsight. Why, even your uncle Vincent remains in the castle to assist during this time. You see, this has been a family affair in your years-long absence. Though the question here is for you. Look around. You have a city of vampires needing guidance, lost humans, helpless women and children in need of a savior. Your poor, delicate mother with the weight of Belladonia on her beautiful back. And yet you refuse the crown? Are you so sure that is the virtuous decision?"

"I don't give a damn about virtue," I replied weakly. But Count Drakon had abilities of his own. He knew my weakness, knew everyone's soft spot, and so often exploited it. Something in me could hardly bear the thought of leaving parents and children scared and lonely, roaming the streets of this place that was not made for them. They had to find a way home. We had to find a way to help them.

My gaze met Ames's. He only sucked in a breath. "I don't know," he answered my unspoken question. "For me, it's always Blythe. I will find a way back to her, regardless of what you choose to do." He looked to the queen and then out the window to the city beyond. "She'll understand. You know she will."

Running my hands through my hair, I looked around the hollow gothic room. The family I'd searched for and the misfit family I'd created for myself. The wicked count looked on haughtily. My mother with sadness and hope. Elysium with his curiosity. And Ames... who knew what he was thinking? There was need for me in Belladonia, and my father wasn't wrong in his assessment that I had a soft spot in my dark heart for women and children.

The castle and its finery perhaps were tempting as well... to call myself a king, to rule my own kingdom, to command the legions of vampires... Well, I don't have to tell you that stroked my pride infinitely. But Blythe, my wife, my belladonna. My werewolf love, my archdemon, the Halloween Boys and Ash Grove. Could I leave them behind, if only for a time? My small cottage and humble farm paled in comparison to the opulence here. The time it would afford me to know my mother, my capacity for good in Belladonia, was astronomical. Would I say no to change in favor of more of the same? My dragon swirled behind my ribs with his preferred answer.

He was right, and I knew what I had to do.

CHAPTER 9

Blythe

THE DEVIL'S IN THE DETAILS

> He was her dark fairytale and she was his twisted fantasy. Together they made magic.
> *F. Scott Fitzgerald*

I wiggled my toes in the plush grass and stretched, feeling the sun warm my cheeks. Looking around, I didn't recognize my surroundings. It was a field filled with bushes. Hadn't I just been asleep in Wolf's house? Standing, I ran my palms over the prickly leaves, feeling them brush my skin, as real as anything. Twirling a deep purple berry between my fingers, I felt its juice stain my skin. Bringing my thumb to my lips, I tasted the sour liquid, when something moved in my periphery.

"How did you know that I adore blackberries?" a low, velvety voice asked.

My heart confused its way through a flutter of passion and a drop of dread as I locked eyes with the devil. "Is this a dream, or is it real?"

He stepped closer, and I realized I'd never seen him in sunlight before. God, he was always breathtaking.

"Yes." He reached a leather gloved hand over my shoulder, and

I trembled at the minor, innocent brush of his wrist. Plucking a few berries, he ate one and smirked. "You're getting better. Strength looks good on you, Reaper. Though you're not nearly as strong as you will be soon."

I didn't have time for his riddles. Somehow, with Judas, I always felt like a mouse between the paws of a cat. The devil was always toying with me, and I never seemed to glean anything meaningful from our encounters, which begged the question of why he even wanted to see me. What did he get from playing with me?

"You said you wanted to get to know me. Back in Belladonia. What do you want to know?"

His eyebrows raised while he inhaled the fresh spring air. "Lace or leather?"

"What? Just like you to throw me off with something stupid like that." I crossed my arms, but I was smiling. And he… he smiled too. Had I ever seen his smile? It was glorious and seductive in its curve and brightness, and the knowing that he didn't share it often, if ever. The realization warmed me with satisfaction that I didn't want but accepted anyway.

"Indulge me."

"Both."

"Could almost be a song, don't you think?" The devil liked Stevie Nicks, too? I was impressed. He took a warm blackberry from his palm and nudged softly between my lips. I froze and heated at the contact but accepted the sugary offering, sucking through the seeds. His intense gaze fell to my mouth. "Meet me here again. You'll know when. And remember to keep my secrets. When you come, I will find you, Mortala."

My response locked in my throat, and someone's hands were around my shoulders, shaking me.

"Blythe?" Wolf's voice was steeped in concern as his rough touch moved from my arms to my hands. "Your hands are freezing." He covered them with his and brought them to his mouth, blowing hot air atop my nails. "I heard your heartbeat slow. It was too slow. I came to wake you, and you wouldn't wake up. You scared the hell out of me."

"Oh," I looked around. It was morning, and I was back in his furs. Or rather, I'd never left. But I'd been with Devil in the black-berry patch. I knew I had. "I guess I was just really tired."

"You've been asleep for two days. I thought you were just catching up on rest until I heard your heart slow. I freaked out." He gave me my hands back and rubbed his stubbled face. "You sure you feel all right? I'm going to make you some rosemary bone broth. That'll help restore your vitality. We drink it before long journeys here at Fenrir."

I nodded. "I'm fine. Don't worry." Was I fine? I wasn't sure, but I was indeed worried. What was happening to me? I wanted to tell him, share where I'd gone and what the devil had said, but I couldn't. Who knew what repercussions there would be if I broke our bargain. Or, I supposed it was possible I did imagine the whole thing. I'd always been a vivid dreamer. Then again, as I'd learned in Belladonia, sometimes what I thought was a dream, or night-mare, was quite real. "Broth sounds nice. I am hungry."

Wolfgang grinned and nodded. "It's an old wolven recipe. I think you'll like it."

I couldn't help my own smile. "Do you like cooking?"

"I love it. There's something special about feeding folks, caring for them, nourishing them. I've wanted to do these things for you for a long time." He rubbed the back of his neck. "Thanks for letting me care for you. I know shit is crazy right now and I'm not exactly in my right mind."

"Raven said you're an alpha werewolf now. What does that mean?"

He stood then and stoked the fire before pausing at the open door. "Nothing good."

After he left, I inspected my hands, knowing what I'd see but feeling the horror of it all the same. My fingertips were stained purple in blackberry juice.

THE NEXT FEW days consisted of Wolfgang feeding me and me sleeping without the intrusion of devil dreams. The mystery man's stupid countdown played in my mind. The one he'd begun in Belladonia. Were we at six or seven? What happened when we reached zero? Would he even hold true to this game or was it just a device to throw me off balance?

Each morning, I hoped to wake up to all my guys around me, but that didn't happen, and I was worried. As Wolfgang presented me with brown pants, hiking boots, and a light long-sleeved top, I laced my shoes and asked, "Are you taking care of me to avoid talking to the mean white luna wolf?"

He snorted, washing a casserole dish. He'd made chicken and rice the night before, and it was divine. I felt selfish lounging in the woods with my werewolf, but his nerves were on a short rope. I wasn't sure what it would take to unleash the alpha half man, half beast again. I didn't want to experience that at the moment, at least not without the guys here. I hoped Ash Grove was okay, and with every bump in the night I heard, I wondered if those creatures were roaming, tormenting someone else.

"I'm not afraid of anyone, least of all a wolf who can't lead," he grumbled, drying his hands on his apron. "Though I will have to talk to them eventually. Today, I guess."

"I'll go with you."

"You'll stay here."

"Boarded up like a kitten in a kennel? No, I don't think so. I can be helpful. Plus, I'm getting cabin fever." I stood and wrapped him in a hug from behind as he stood at the sink. He froze. My arms didn't even reach all the way around him, he was so wide. I loved the size of my great and powerful Wolf. "Don't you want to explore? Maybe we can find the guys. Maybe we can check on Ash Grove?"

He let out a long sigh. "My mood is very… tenuous right now. If anything threatened you, or if another man or wolf even looked at you for too long, I'm afraid I'd rip them apart right then and there."

"How's that going to work when the guys are here?" I asked, unsure of what to do with his sudden influx of jealous behavior.

He shrugged. "I guess I'll kick their asses for a bit. They deserve it for one reason or another. But we're all mated, so I don't expect I'll have to beat them too hard."

I giggled. "Boys."

Putting a big arm around my shoulder, Wolf agreed that I could join him in Fenrir. We walked through the freshly cut grass around his house, which I guessed he'd done when I'd been sleeping for days, and into the main open field of Fenrir. Three kids ran by, laughing as they floated a kite behind them. A few women and young folks sat on the big logs around the main fire pit. They stood as Wolfgang approached, and I noticed the white wolf was among them. Her braided pale hair was pulled back in a low bun, and she held a power of authority around her, despite Wolf believing her to be weak.

"I trust you and your mate are rested now," she said, offering me a small smile. "I do apologize for my previous behavior. You must realize we've been through so much. Many tricks and phantoms have haunted our every move."

"It's okay," I offered. "I'm Blythe Pearl."

"Nice to meet you, I'm Nephele." She looked hesitantly to Wolf, who did not exude the warmth he usually did as he stood with crossed arms. "I can get you up to speed on Fenrir happenings, since you are part of the leadership as an alpha now."

"Blythe is more forgiving than I am, and you're lucky to have her mercy. If you didn't, I would have killed you all. I've yet to decide if I'm taking on this pack."

"You must," Nephele argued. "You're the alpha we were promised. You come from Fenrir. This is your destiny. Your werewolf form isn't merely strong. It's intuitive, with spirit gifts you can only imagine—"

"I'm not joining your headship of a scrawny pack. For all I

know, you're all lying enemy wolves who killed the elders and lunas and did a shitty job commanding Fenrir and this land in their absence."

Nephele gritted her teeth and held fists at her side. "You dare say such a thing to me? Where've you been, huh? Where were you when your wolven needed you, Wolfgang Jack?"

Her tone made me cringe as I dared a look up at Wolf, who furrowed his brow and took a seat on one of the massive tree trunks. "You get one opportunity to tell me what happened and convince me otherwise."

I took my place on the log next to him, waiting as Nephele paced in front of the fire, a very canine thing to do, before she stared at her feet and spoke. "First the phantom circus approached us. They asked for Fenrir's land and threatened to take it by force. Of course, we didn't allow that. Though to garner peace, we offered them a portion of the woods, as long as no humans were harmed in their activities. All seemed fine for a time, before the bat creatures descended. The witches' wards protected most of the people of Ash Grove, though our own boundaries did not antici-pate their arrival, and their smell was that of any bat or vampire to us. Still, we lost no wolves in their attack, remarkably. After enforcing our borders and protections, the ghouls came. In numbers like never before. Calliach and the elders decided to travel north, over the mountain and through the woods. In search of aid. When they did not return, the lunas went looking for them."

Wolf tensed next to me, and I put my hand atop his in gentle support. But my own fear was creeping in, and I was afraid to listen to more.

Nephele continued. "As you can guess, the lunas did not return. Leaving me, an adolescent at the time, and—"

"Me," a large man with red hair and a long red beard inter-rupted. "I'm Carmine. We met a long time ago, Wolfgang, when I was a pup."

Wolf gave him a short nod and glanced back to Nephele. "Continue."

"I've spoken to the pack; it seems many of the adolescents remember you. I am newer to Fenrir, having been a young lone wolf who'd not found this pack until after you had left, so again, I apologize for my ignorance in not knowing who you were." She sighed. "With our numbers diminished, we worked around the clock, hunting ghouls and contending with the new blood-sucking creatures. The witch coven in Ash Grove was little help, as they were going through their own issues at the time and could not lend much assistance in addition to warding Ash Grove against the new evils. But the worst had yet to happen at that point."

The wolves looked to the grass, sorrow pulling their features. Carmine stood and put a gentle hand on Nephele's back. She tensed her jaw, avoiding our gaze, and after a moment, the red wolf continued for her. "The phantom of the circus came to us with a deal. Fenrir in exchange for eradicating the beasts."

Wolf huffed, and his breathing was heavy. He was angry, so angry. I rubbed his knuckles softly, hoping to offer him some measure of calm, but even my own heart was racing at the story being told.

"We denied them. And then..." Carmine shook his head. "Then the pups began disappearing."

"The pups?" Wolf growled in furious disbelief. "How?"

"We don't know," Nephele said with a shaky voice. "Believe me, you cannot shame us more than we have ourselves. We did everything, followed every rule, every point of guardianship. We currently are left with four pups and one pregnant luna. Our pack is but a little over a dozen wolven now."

It fell silent in the grassy knoll and the spring woods beyond. Wolfgang rested his elbows on his knees and stared at the dirt. I could almost hear his racing thoughts, his disappointment mixed with what I knew was a strong urge to protect and lead his pack. I wished I could help him.

After a moment, he looked up at the two standing before him. "What aid did the elders go in search of?"

Carmine glanced at Nephele, who replied with a steely voice. "The Halloween Boys. And you."

CHAPTER 10
Wolf

HIS LONESOME WILDERNESS

> We ran off as if to meet the moon.
> *Robert Frost*

With every beat of my axe, another set of eyes bored into my soul. The earnest and innocent gaze of a pack forgotten, abandoned, torn to shreds. It was all my fucking fault. A rumble shook the misty forest before I realized it was my own cry of rage. The tree cracked and shook, twigs and branches falling before it tumbled forward. My run in my beast form had taken me past the border of daffodils. A party trick, a tiny laughable protection against terrors that, when we were at full strength as a pack, would never dare come near with or without bewitched flora. Fenrir was like a house made of straw, and the big bads of our world were huffing and puffing and all but blowing the house down.

And they all looked to me. In hope, in disappointment, in fright. My abdomen and chest burned as I took my fury out on the fallen maple. Wood. I'd supply them with wood. I'd get this burning and agonizing failure out of my system by obliterating something. Stopping mid-swing, I inhaled deeply the sap riddled air, hoping I sensed what I thought I did. Where the hell were Ghost and Onyx?

I couldn't let Blythe see my trepidation. She'd already seen enough of the insanity and insecurity I so carefully concealed from the world. Hundreds of years' worth of stealthy carnivore instinct bred a shield of invisibility. Happy, pleasant, caring house dog. That's who I was, or who I wanted to be, or maybe only what they thought I was. But it wasn't the whole truth, was it?

I was a beast of halves even worse than Onyx. The vampire-dragon at least adhered to consent. My darkest truth? The way I felt with my maw wrapped around Blythe's neck. In that moment, I didn't want to stop. I didn't care what she thought or if she wanted me like I wanted her. All the unleashed alpha werewolf desired was to fuck her raw. To spill my seed into her aromatic, delicious pussy. To have and own her womb and breed her. The knot at the base of my cock would ensure that fantasy come to fruition.

Just the thought of locking my cum inside her, feeling her hips shake at the long intrusion… through my rush of emotions, an erection tensed against my jeans. Adjusting myself, tucking it into my waistband and telling it to shut the fuck up, I slung the axe over my bare shoulder and turned, feeling sweat drip from down my neck.

Blythe hugged her knees, watching with wide eyes and rosy cheeks from atop a mossy boulder. Her scent only made my cock throb harder, and I imagined how both of her forearms could fit so easily in one of my hands when I pinned them above her head. God, her fragrance had afflicted me since the moment she arrived in Ash Grove.

I remembered the first time I smelled her. I'd fixated on her scent for days before I'd even met her. Until I finally had to hunt her down. That day, I found her. Peering through brush in the woods behind her old apartment, I watched her. She listened to music while scattering peanuts for birds, and I was mesmerized by her. The lunas had always taught me, *Trust your nose. Your eyes and ears will play tricks on you, but smell never lies.* Blythe smelled like starlight. I realize that's a stupid thing to say, but something about her smelled like the darkness in the first chill of October. Somber in all its breathtaking beauty. Her scent suited her, and it drew me to her like a werewolf to the full moon.

She swallowed, pulling her gaze from my body and meeting my stare. Onyx would have something clever and flirtatious to say in this situation. He'd have her laughing like he always did. Ghost would have his hand down her pants and fingers in her cunt instead of gawking and avoiding her touch as I was. So instead, I kicked a log and apologized for throwing her on my back and taking off into the woods. She'd ridden on my back as a wolf before, when I'd gotten her away from the legion of demons in October. I liked the feel of her grip on my fur. I knew I couldn't leave her in Fenrir, not alone. Even if the forest was infested with monster filth, she was still safer with me, and my werewolf wouldn't let her out of his sight, regardless.

"It's okay," she assured, picking at a dandelion. "That meeting was intense, but I hope you know it's not your fault. None of this is on you."

I huffed. "You are a very compassionate and forgiving person, Blythe. But what I did, abandoning my pack for so long, intentional or not, this *is* on me. If I'm to join the lunas as an alpha, I can't start the gig by not taking the blame that's owed to me. If I'd been here, none of this shit would have happened."

"You don't know that."

"I would have died before letting Fenrir fall." I sucked in a shaking breath. "The elders... pups... goddamn pups gone. Snatched away like coyotes preying on baby lambs. And I wasn't here."

"We can fix it," she pressed. "Nephele says Ash Grove is fine enough. I'll find Yesenia. The guys will find their way back to us. We'll put it all back together again."

My chest constricted in longing for my wide-eyed, hopeful mate. But she couldn't help, and this was on me alone. But what the hell did I know about being an alpha? I'd been comfortable letting the lunas do their job. Likewise, I'd let Ghost and Devil be the authority of the Halloween Boys. My pack, my family, they were all each to me. Fenrir and my guys were my life, and now Blythe was a part of that, too. And what a shit show I'd brought her into. Not the introduction to wolf culture and the celebration of Laverna that I'd planned and dreamed of.

I wiped the sweat from my brow while a fresh wave of the honeysuckle incense of her arousal burned my nose, and I snapped. "Would you stop smelling like that?"

"Do I stink?" Blythe shrieked, sliding off the rock, the motion drawing my attention to her wide hips. Perfect for every bit of the pummeling I wanted to give her. "You're the one who insisted on a milk and rose bath or whatever that was. Excuse me if I haven't found any suitable perfume in Fenrir—"

I crossed the distance with a huff, and she backed up a step, like she was running, a slight motion that meant nothing to humans but everything to a predator. A predator, a wolf like me. She gasped, her sarcasm dying on her lips, as I leaned against the rock, boxing her in.

"You smell good enough to eat. That's the problem," I growled, burrowing my nose into her hair. Her dainty palms pushed against my chest as I pressed my hips against her soft stomach. "I want to put my baby there. Right there."

"Wolf," she breathed, pushing against me a little more.

"Something you don't know about me is that I'm a sick fuck and think it's hot when you try to push me off. When you run or fight me, it'll only make it worse. Make me fuck you harder."

Suddenly, my hand was around her neck. Not my hand. No, the half man, half beast's hand. The werewolf's long paw and limber claws. I hadn't gotten to play in this form yet, but I liked that I had fingers and padding and claws. My body felt stronger than ever before as a were. Like the most formidable and useful parts of a wolf combined with a man to make me a superhuman, an advanced canine, and hungry for her.

"I can't breathe when you do that," she choked out. "Your claws kind of hurt. I'm not entirely sure whether you'll fatally harm me." Her little hand stroked my jaw. I loosened my grip, and the claws and massive grip on her neck shrank.

I pressed my forehead against the cool rock above her. "This must be terrible for you. I'm so sorry, Blythe. I'm so sorry for what I am."

Surprise flitted through me at the feel of her wrapping around my middle. "It's not terrible at all. I'm actually… quite intrigued about this dark side of my moon boy."

A rough, unexpected chuckled rumbled through me. "Moon boy? You've definitely been hanging around Onyx too long." I straightened, happy to see her answering smile, and extended my hand, my human hand. "Come with me. I want to show you some-place secret."

She raised a curious eyebrow. "What if those creepy monsters find us? We've already been out here a while."

I snorted. "I hope they do. I'd love to tear a few more apart right now." But just in case, I tilted my head to the sky and let out a howl, informing the pack of what needed to be done. If they even knew how. Then the fresh sadness washed over me again. They were ill-equipped, and much of that was my fault.

Her fingers laced with mine. "I'd follow you anywhere."

CHAPTER 11

Blythe

MOON SONG

It was love at first sight, at last sight, at ever and ever sight.

Vladimir Nabokov

Dusk painted the woods in deep orange and creamy purple as we trekked up a steep, winding path. Wolf's shoulders visibly relaxed the farther up the mountain we went. I wondered if it meant we were getting farther from the monsters that plagued the Fenrir, or if nature relaxed him more than anything else. Pausing, I thumbed at a fuzzy plant, and he noticed, smiling.

"Lamb's Ear. I used to pet them, too, on my walks up here as a pup."

"It does look like a lamb's ear." I giggled. "So, this secret spot is from Wolfgang-Pup's childhood?"

He chuckled, the sound like sweet molasses as he took my hand, helping me up the last big step. As we turned the corner, I inhaled the wet air as it breezed through my hair.

"My grandfather took me fishing up here all the time. Some of the biggest fish you'll find right beneath the waterfall."

The waterfall crashed and raged white amongst an otherwise

tranquil lake, cocooned by smooth rocks and greenery. It seemed to be twinkling in the twilight. No... it *was* twinkling. "It sparkles?" I squealed like a kid, eliciting another blessed chuckle.

"That's only one part of its magic."

"Why didn't I know this existed so close to Ash Grove?" I asked, tugging off my boots and dipping a toe into the cool water.

"You don't think I have my own secrets from the Halloween Boys? I'm hurt you think me so innocent."

Wolf unbuttoned his pants, and I looked away, hiding my flush. "I guess I did think of you as a sort of cinnamon roll. You're so sweet and you make me feel so safe."

His bare chest and abdomen pressed against my back as he reached around, gently tugging at my shirt. "It's true that I value kindness more so than my crew." I lifted my arms, and he peeled my shirt away, leaving me topless in the spring air. His big, rough hands lightly grazed the soft flesh atop my ribs and down my plush stomach, freezing the breath within me and sending every bit of heat in my body rushing between my thighs. When he unbuttoned my pants for me, I couldn't contain my panting. It seemed he'd been teasing me forever. "But there's a beast within..." He took my earlobe between his teeth and pulled gently. "And I think you know he's starving for you."

I kicked off my pants and pushed at my panties, feeling the heat of his hips and the strength of his length pushing into my back. His grip found my wrist, and he whispered roughly, "Leave those on."

He moved around me in that stealthy, lupine way that told my basic instincts that he was a predator. His earlier words about me being afraid of him weren't wrong. Well, not afraid exactly. More so aware. The keen awareness that my lovers were lethal sent thrills of excitement through me. I never knew what to expect from Ghost, Dragon, or Wolf. And I was enjoying seeing this side of my gentle giant. Disappointment cooled me, along with the water, when I noticed Wolfgang didn't remove his form-fitting boxer briefs. Instead, he took me by the waist and eased me into the water, laughing as I wiggled against the chill.

"Can you swim?" he asked, grinning in that heart-melting, panty-dropping way of his. He was always touching me, since the moment we met, we'd had a sort of magnetism, and I always wanted to be touching him, too. I was comfortable with Wolf in a way I hadn't experienced so quickly with anyone else. I rubbed playfully at his scruffy cheeks.

"I can only doggy paddle. You should appreciate that, hmm?"

Wolfgang's laughter rivaled the thunderous falls next to us, and despite the chilly lake, I warmed at knowing I'd brought him a moment of happiness, of relief, from our plight at Fenrir.

"Hold on to my neck. I'll swim us up to the falls," he instructed, shrugging me around him. I nuzzled his back and took in his warmth and strength. "Don't doggy paddle too hard. There are all sorts of critters that bite in this lake."

I yelped, wrapping my legs around his trunk.

He chuckled again. "I thought you liked being bitten by our boy."

A giggle left my lips as the water from the falls pelted us as we swam to the underside of it. "Our boy," I repeated. "I like that. I miss them. We've all been apart for too long."

"I agree." Wolf lifted me by my shoulders onto a slick slab of earth hidden behind the raging white water.

"This is beautiful," I breathed, wringing out my long hair. The water had also felt nice on my sore muscles, which were feeling stronger by the day.

From behind me again, Wolf pressed his callused finger against my lips, while the other arm wrapped around me, harboring me in the heat of his large body. "Shh… watch and listen."

It was hard to watch or listen to anything while feeling him against my back and hips and ass. But suddenly, I heard it and saw it and understood what he meant. A flute-like whistling floated through the air. It should have been impossible to hear, and its human-tone should have rendered it silenced by the falls, but it echoed through the tiny enclave and pierced the air sharper than the pouring water.

Alongside the whistle of a melody, colors erupted around us. Blues, greens, pinks, and reds cascaded down the underside of the waterfalls, rippling with the water. The hues of bright colors danced with the song, and I put a hand to my mouth and tilted my head to look at Wolf. Who, instead of looking at the extraordinary, magical show before us, was looking at me.

"What is this?" I whispered as our eyes locked and my cheeks flushed from the intensity in his stare.

"Some call her the spirit of the water. Or the witch of the water. She whistles at dusk and dawn, and every now and then, if she likes you, she'll put on a little show." He turned me around to face him. "I guess she's helping me out tonight."

He lowered, so soft, so gentle, and stopped before my lips. An offering, or maybe an asking of permission. Butterflies erupted in my chest as I closed the distance, kissing him, relishing the feel of his bristles as they scratched my chin. His tongue ever so kindly parted my kiss and mingled with mine. If Ghost's kiss was honey, and Onyx's wine, Wolfgang's was a peach warmed by the sun in July. As our breathing picked up, he pulled back, searching my gaze. A kaleidoscope of blues lit his face, and I could again hear the music from the witch of the water.

"This is how I wanted our first time to be," he confessed. "I imagined spoiling you in Fenrir and then bringing you here. Showing you the falls and the aurora colors." He tucked a wet strand of hair behind my ear, and I leaned into his palm. "Don't get me wrong; I've loved every piece of you I've gotten over these past few months. I've gotten to watch you, care for you, protect you. And recently, I've gotten to taste and feel you, though for far too briefly."

"Let's remedy that now," I suggested, standing on my tiptoes and kissing him again. He leaned against the rock wall, and it seemed a little ridiculous that I was the one trying to pin him in. "What's the matter? Don't you want me?" I asked, fighting with the insecurity that wanted to fester. He cared for me, and he was obviously attracted to me, but why was he moving so slowly right now?

He rubbed my arms and eyed my bare breasts before looking at me through a darker gaze. "Because I want our first time alone to be you and me. Not me as, you know, the werewolf. Though he'll want his turn, too." That entire statement made me wetter than the swim ever could have. "I want your first real time with me to leave you feeling loved and secure in my feelings for you, Blythe." He kissed my jaw as a hand trailed up my stomach, parting my breasts before gripping my throat. "Because you might doubt that once I fuck you as an alpha. Understand?"

Words. What were words again? I only managed a nod.

"And you probably noticed during the blood ritual that my… you know… works a little differently than—"

"Wolfgang," I interrupted in a whine, a plea of desperation. I only just caught his brief smirk before he lifted me and turned us around, pinning me to the wet rock of reds turning to pinks. His mouth covered mine again, only this time, his kiss was deeper, fuller, and everything I wanted. I moaned onto his tongue as his palm found my breast, moving his roughness over my aching nipple. His other hand hooked behind my knee, opening my legs. I could feel his hard shaft slide against my cold, drenched panties, and in the midst of our kissing, I slid my touch over his firm abdomen, down to tug at the waistband of his boxers. He broke our kiss with a wolfish grin.

"I like leaving them on."

I giggled as he dropped to kiss my neck. But my laughter turned to a moan as his rough fingers pushed under my panties and dipped into my wanting sex. "You're going to leave yours on, too. I want all of this." He pushed two fingers inside me, and my forehead fell against his shoulder at the glorious intrusion. "Every bit of your arousal soaked into the fabric is like my own personal sex toy. It's mine." He pushed a third finger in, and I cried out as he pumped at a steady pace. "This pussy, these panties, this wetness; it's mine."

My orgasm fell with the falls and danced with the color show around us. I hadn't even registered that he'd pinned my wrists above me with one hand until his teeth toyed with my nipples, bringing me down from my release and back into his fairy-tale erotic world. My breasts tingled at every swipe of his tongue and nip of his teeth until I was writhing against him and the wet stone wall behind me. Stopping, he lifted his three fingers to his lips and sucked them clean, one by one. "Honeysuckle in summertime," he growled, tasting my bliss on his skin.

I let my palms explore his pectoral muscles and chest hair before getting lost in his kiss again. "Make love to me, Wolfgang," I asked sweetly in his ear. My giant, my raging beast of a man who could have had me in the graveyard, who could have fucked me senseless as I lay bruised and tired in his house, waited. Beyond that, he'd waited as Ghost claimed me and as Dragon snatched me away. My patient defender had wanted to make sure I was okay. He wanted to ensure that it was romantic. And it was. This was romance of princess proportions, and my werewolf lord was everything I could have wanted. I wanted to be everything for him, too. Somehow, I'd figure out a way to be what he needed, too.

With a growl low in his throat that wasn't wholly human, he reached between us and jerked the waistband of his briefs under his length. I admired his size and wondered at what he was trying to tell me about it before I interrupted with my sex-crazed impatience. But it didn't matter, especially not when he pulled my panties to the side and lined up with my opening. I held on to his neck as his thick, rounded tip pressed in.

"So deliciously wet for me," he praised. "What a good girl you are."

My head fell back, and we groaned together as he sank in halfway, stretching me, filling me, consuming me from the inside out. "I don't remember what happened at the end of the blood ritual," I panted, twisting my hips as I took him fully inside me.

"Let me remind you," he rumbled, then retreated and slammed back into me. My cries echoed along the cave, and our joined sounds slicked with the water around us. His girth was huge and wonderful and making me see stars with every stroke in and out. The edge of my panties pulled and strained against my clit in a frustrating build with every move he made. Then his grip returned to my throat and my pussy clenched around him. "Fuck, you like when I do that, don't you?"

I nodded, wrapping a hand around his wrist and begging his grip to tighten. The trust I had with Wolf invited endless possibilities of sexual play. He could do whatever he wanted to me, and I knew he'd be listening to my body and caring for my soul as we did it. He squeezed his hand around my neck and pushed into the lingering bruises from his maw, mixed with Onyx's bites, and my ecstasy exploded around us. The lack of oxygen emptied my mind, and all that was left was the pleasure, the slick and tight feel of him as he picked up his pace, pummeling me with his cock, squeezing my neck as I rode out my orgasm.

With a primal roar, his hand constricted around my throat as the other one dug into my hip, pricking the skin, and I knew it was a struggle not to let the werewolf free. But now my body was so thoroughly fucked up by being fucked by monsters that pain and pleasure danced a dangerously close line. The welts from his claws, or Onyx's bites, or Ghost's enormous cock, were what I craved now. How could I ever accept the subpar touch of a human man? I never had, and I knew I never would.

Our groans married with the melody of the water spirits and blurred with the rainbow prisms dancing in the cave. And then, suddenly, I gasped at the stretch. The massive stretch and fullness inside me. It reminded me instantly of my first time with Ames on his grave, when he shifted as we were having sex. Was Wolf doing the same? I looked up, not finding the answer in his amber gaze, as he only kissed me deeply while the stretch widened and intensified.

I cried out in another wave of blissful agony while another

unexpected release trembled through my body. Wolfgang remained still, pinning me against the cave, the fullness not retreating in the slightest. When I could form words, I managed a strained inquiry as to what was happening, and his rough, sex-toned voice responded.

"I'm knotting you, Blythe. Feel that burn? It's keeping my cum inside you for as long as I want it to be. I told you; you're all mine. Your womb is mine to fill and ensure it stays full of me."

"God, why is that so fucking hot?" I panted, wiggling against the sensation and feeling his hot cum locked within the stretch with no escape. "I don't even want kids," I let out, not so delicately.

He smiled and bit at my ear. "That's fine. I want what you want. But the fantasy is fun to indulge, and breeding is a big fucking kink of mine."

"I like it, too," I admitted. I'd had no idea I liked it until then. Until earlier, when he talked about filling me with his babies. In reality, it wasn't something I wanted, or could probably even do as, you know, Death incarnate. But as a sexy fantasy, the thought was really hot.

He held me close as my walls adjusted to him, and instead of being impatient or moving on to the next matter of business, I let him hold me, and I held him back. My lips lazily grazed his skin, tasting soil and maple. Then my hands raked through his wavy hair and twirled the curls between my fingers. Wolf peppered my jaw with kisses. Every move he made was one of awe and worship as he lightly cupped my breasts and kneaded at my thighs. Where the beginning of our encounter was about passion and desire, as I remained quite literally locked against him, his knot uniting us as one, these touches were those of admiration and care as we explored each other's bodies with reverent curiosity.

And in the colors and water and the song lifting around us. I could have stayed there with him. Knot or no knot, we were perfect the way we were.

CHAPTER 12

Wolf

LAMB'S EAR

> Where there is life there is hope.
> *J.R.R. Tolkien*

I'd been alive a long time, and instead of focusing on the grimmer aspects of that existence, as my friends so often did. Nights like the one I'd just had reminded me of all the magic that exists in the world. And not the magic of witches and devils and wolves, but an even realer, truer sort of magic. The kind that comes about with someone you love. The quiet in the cave, buried in Blythe, was the most divine moment of my life so far.

And somehow, despite my mistakes and the guilt heavy on my back, life had given me a moment of wonder with her. One that was deserving and worthy of everything she was. She didn't only deserve romance; she required it. And I'd give her nothing less. It would be different when I shifted. When the full moon came and turned me into an uncontrollable raging beast again, I wouldn't be romancing her tenderly. This was important. It was vital she knew my true feelings and care before she fully experienced that side of me, the alpha. My alpha was a ticking bomb, and the full moon was weeks away.

We reached the other side of the lake to an unwelcome surprise.

"Where are my clothes?" Blythe shrieked, searching through the bushes.

I rubbed my neck, hoping the darkness that was falling and the lights fading concealed my grin. "In exchange for the show, the spirits usually take them."

"I'm naked!" She yelped. "I can't walk into Fenrir topless and in wet panties."

"Those panties are mine now, remember? And you're in pack territory now. Wolves adapt, with or without clothes."

"Not the time for jokes." She stomped her foot.

I found a dogwood tree and pulled a T-shirt from its branches. "Don't worry. I have a shirt stashed… no pants, though."

She jerked it from my hold. "You're lucky you're so cute, Wolfgang Jack."

I pulled her close, breathing in and smelling the top of her hair. "Say my name like that again, and I'll swim you right back under the falls for round two."

As I slipped my big shirt over her head and she nuzzled my warmth, my nose tingled in awareness, and I caught the paws and claws as they neared. Blythe startled when she heard them, too late, and turned. She was so ill-equipped to defend herself. How could I ever let her out of my sight? If these had been threats, she would have been pounced before she ever realized their approach.

Three wolves, adolescent males, or sols, as we called them in pack world, looked up at us with big gray eyes that matched their pelts.

I asked, "I take it you came to escort us back? And the lunas are with the pack?"

They nodded. "Yes, sir. I'm Remi, and this is Apollo and Skyler. No threats on the way up. Maybe they smell you and are leaving us alone."

I snorted. "If they were smart, we could guess as much. Though I don't think these creatures are intelligent."

"It's nice to meet you, Remi, Apollo, and Skyler. I'm Blythe," she squeaked after a moment, shocking us all at once.

I looked to her, raising my brows. "You heard them? Only wolves and demons can hear other wolves in their canine form."

She shrugged.

"Let's head out. It's getting dark." I rubbed my jaw, mulling over her revelation as she slipped on her boots. Then we carefully followed the wolves down the mountain. My keen wolfish sight that saw as plainly at night as it did during the day should have been scanning the woods. Instead, I was watching for glimpses of her ass cheeks as she stepped down the steep pathway wearing only my T-shirt. It was begging for me to rip it off her and bend her over. If it wasn't for the young sols around us, I would have. That is until we heard panting and smelled swamp and decay. The young wolves stopped and raised their ears, baring their teeth. I had to decide in that moment how best to protect my mate, a situation I hadn't encountered alone, though I'd learned a great deal from watching Ghost and Onyx in these situations.

Ghost shielded her as he fought. Onyx, I imagined, did the same with his fire. My gifts didn't afford any supernatural barriers of protection except for my pack...

"Encircle Blythe," I commanded lowly.

"What's going on?" She looked around, confused. "Oh, no, I smell it. I hate these things."

I'd never been approached by a ghoul. On the contrary, werewolves had to hunt them down and smoke them out of their hiding places like rats from a sewer. And the other creatures, the warped vampires from Belladonia, shouldn't have even been here. Something wasn't right. Even with the monsters plaguing us. And why Fenrir? Nephele had mentioned the chaos magicians, yet they weren't the ones stalking us through the woods right now, were they?

The sols did as they were told, and Blythe was surrounded by a cloud of thick gray fur. They may have been teenagers, but they were large, coming up to her waist on all fours. But I hadn't trained them myself and didn't know their skill in fighting yet. I chose to take this on myself. And wolves never ran. We stood our ground and took our opponents head-on.

A voice whispered from its hiding place. "We chase you now. How the tables have turned, werewolf."

It was in a talking mood. Odd. "You actively and foolishly seek death, then, ghoul."

"In fact, yes. Hand Death over, and we will leave."

I froze in place, its hiss raising the hairs on the back of my neck. "What did you say?"

The ghoul appeared like a mirage coming into focus. Around it were four more, and behind them, shook and screeched the diphylla. At least six. I glanced back at the wolves who snarled in response, baring their teeth. Blythe's heart rate was through the roof, and the smell of her fear was so powerful I could barely restrain myself from ripping the creature's throats then and there.

The ghoul whispered again, a chill on the night air. "Give us the girl. We know you have her, though we cannot see her. We know she travels with you."

They couldn't see her. That's right. Death was always hidden. Just as the Halloween boys couldn't sense her when she'd arrived in Ash Grove. That had changed now, though, hadn't it? Another mystery to sort through around a campfire with the guys. I wondered how much I could get out of this abnormally chatty ghoul before they struck.

"Who sent you?"

It hissed and moved forward. "We will kill each of you. Each wolf and its young, every human, until she is all that's left."

It was the first time I wished for my alpha wolf form. It could only be fully accessed nearer the full moon, and I had weeks between me and that damn moon, so my shadow beast form would have to suffice. I'd killed hundreds of these things—though something in the way they spoke and approached us was strange and had me hesitant to underestimate them, even if they were lowly forest scum. A diphylla lunged, and the sols behind me howled. Remi pounced, ripping the vampire creature's neck open.

My paws slammed into the earth as I shouted an order to return to Blythe.

"You can't take them all on your own! Let us fight," the sol argued before he obeyed. I didn't have time to babysit them or make him bleed for disobeying and mouthing off. Two ghouls dug their poisoned talons into my shoulders. Fuck, that was annoying. I dislocated one's head and swiftly snapped the other's neck before three diphylla attacked me at once. The wolves behind me howled, and there was a scuffle of movement. Two were fighting, and I caught sight of Blythe retreating to hide behind a tree as a diphylla sank its fangs into my neck. The pain shot through me and ignited my rage. The lunas would come, what lunas were left anyway, but they'd be too late. I gained the high ground, burying my claws into the diphylla's ribs as a ghoul jumped onto my back, scraping its barbed talons along my underside.

I didn't know what to tell Blythe to do. When I was in my alpha form, I knew she should run to Fenrir, but now, the sense of clarity was fading with the poison of the beasts inching into my bloodstream. Skyler yelped, and Apollo snarled, taking down the ghoul that had injured his friend. But there were so many still, like more were coming to their aid, fearless of the wolves. This had never happened before; this was all wrong.

As I ripped out a throat, two more diphylla charged me, and through the swamp smell and blood I caught the faintest whiff of what was coming for us. An evil much greater than what was between my teeth.

A howl tore through me as blue smoke creeped along the forest floor. It began reaching, pulling, and burning. Diphyllas and ghouls alike began screaming in pain. I straightened, feeling my blood drip down my sides and mat my fur. Taking the opportunity my friend had given me, I finished off two more ghouls as they tried to flee, snapping necks in quicker deaths than they deserved. The archdemon stalked out of the trees and wrapped a ghoul in ropes of smoke. It shrieked and wrestled futilely against Ghost's grip, baring its teeth.

Ghost's low demon voice commanded, "Your life has one purpose now; do you hear me?" The ropes clasped, and the ghoul contorted, shrieking and nodding. "You will go and tell your master that I'm here and he better come find me before I find him. Because I will find him, and I will leave a path of ghoul blood behind me as I do."

Hell smoke lifted the creature and flung it into the forest with a thump of breaking branches. And everything fell quiet again, except for the sounds of the sols licking their wounds and padding through gore over to us.

"Thanks for stopping by." I looked up at my friend. "Took you long enough."

"I was stuck in vampire hell," he growled, his eyes roaming the carnage. "Blythe, is she in Fenrir?"

I shifted back into a man, feeling my core ache and fresh cuts begin to heal, though I was covered in more of my own blood than I would have liked. Panic seized me when I didn't smell her. The sols sniffed and looked at each other and at Ghost and me.

"She didn't run. We would have heard her. We had to fight. We couldn't not fight anymore. There were too many," Remi let out as he anxiously paced. The other sols were sniffing furiously at the tree she was stationed at during the small battle.

Ghost grabbed my throat. "You lost her?"

CHAPTER 13

Blythe

VEILED KINGDOM

I often consider myself as a figure in a foggy painting: faltering lines, insecure distances, and a merging of greys and blacks. An emotion or a mood—a mere wisp of color—is shaded off and made to spread until it becomes one with all that surrounds it.

Virginia Woolf

It was in the middle of watching Wolf's blood gush down his ribs. The fear was so great, but so was my frustration. I wanted to help, needed to do something. The ghouls said they wanted me. I was still being hunted, like I'd always been. Something, someone, was leaving destruction in its wake in its quest to get to me. And as I shuddered behind an oak tree, the sounds of snapping bones, canine sneers, hisses, and shrill gargles of monsters, something whistled in the woods beyond. A sweet, harmonious sound so at odds with what was happening. Then a faint glowing light snaked a pathway.

The whistling stopped, and something lithe giggled in the distance. "Come on now," it whispered, the color changing from gold to green to blue, the same way the hues of the waterfall had. I followed the pathway before me, leaving the fighting behind. The whistling grew nearer, and suddenly it was dawn. Or was it twilight? Not enough time had passed for the sun to have risen. The light was a pale violet glow, and the woods felt different, though they looked the same. "Come, you can sit with me." The voice sounded from a tree with a rounded middle and a slight opening. Wolf and I had hiked this way, but I hadn't noticed a tree like this. It was peculiar and oddly shaped. I glanced over my shoulder, knowing I wasn't far from Wolf. A stick-like hand appeared in the crook of the tree and waved me forward. Taking tentative steps toward it, I kneeled at the base, looking inside the trunk to see a round and spacious little dwelling not at all matching the modest size of the twisted little tree. Climbing inside, I stood upright and looked around, catching the gaze of a pair of big, round jade eyes.

"You can stay with me as long as you like. It can get over-whelming out there," it said in a light tone. The being looked as if it was carved from bark and was small and covered in ivy. It leaned in the curve of the hollow space, holding its knees.

"What are you doing here?" I asked, feeling immediately like that was a stupid question. But I was disoriented and dazed, and this place was so warm and inviting. I didn't get the sense that this creature meant me any harm.

"Learnin' stuff," it said simply. "You're about to go someplace, aren't you? Be easier if you travel through this side of the veil, though. Lots of strange folks here, too."

"This side of the veil? What is that?"

"You know," it said, settling into its nook and closing its eyes. "The part they can't see. The fun part."

"Are you a spirit?" This being reminded me of the willow spirit in a way, and my heart ached in remembrance. They had the same pairing of ancient mixed with youthful innocence that didn't exist in the mortal world. But it was no use; the bark- and plant-covered little thing was snoring as if I wasn't even standing inside its home.

The other side of the veil, it had said. I mulled over its words and oddities as I climbed out of the tree and followed the soft grass and hazy air back in the direction I'd come from. The violet haze faded with each step and darkness greeted me, a heavy, forbidding sense of doom and disaster. It felt awful. Was this how it always felt here? Or was it a contrast to the light I'd just felt in the nook of a tree with a nameless spirit? I found the tree I'd been hiding behind when something silver flashed in my periphery, knocking me to the ground. The wolf howled, and before I could even sit up, I was scooped into big, inky colored arms. I wrapped myself around his neck, choking on a laugh or a sob, I wasn't sure.

"Is Wolf okay?" was all I could get out.

"I'm fine. Don't worry, little one," his rough timbre soothed.

Ghost scanned me from top to bottom, his blue eyes searching until he was satisfied that I was okay. "Where were you?"

"I don't know," I answered honestly.

Wolf interrupted. "We need to get back to Fenrir. Now. There are more coming."

"What the fuck is going on?" Ghost growled, but we were all moving, and he wasn't letting me go. But I was more than okay to finally be back in the embrace of my archdemon. Now I only needed…

I sat up, interrupting their somber communications as the wolves trotted next to us. "Where's Onyx?"

Ghost only grunted in response.

We'd reached Fenrir, and I breathed a sigh of relief as I was gently placed on the porch of Wolfgang's house.

My demon resumed his human form, and it was almost too much seeing him standing next to Wolfgang. They were both so beautiful, otherworldly, and mine. All mine.

Ames pulled on a pair of black sweatpants before tugging me to his chest and tilting my chin up in that sexy and commanding way of his. "A kiss for your archdemon should always be the first thing on your lips."

My cheeks hurt from a smile as his kiss moved atop mine. "You said you'd never leave me again," I teased, breathless when he pulled away.

"It wasn't by choice, but I'll fight the universe and its cruelty later." He smirked, and my heart thawed. That same curl of black hair, the same tint of blue in his icy stare. My Ames Cove, my Ghost. I wrapped myself in his arms as he kissed my hair. "Glad to see Wolf has left you in one piece."

"He has. He's been very good." I smiled, glancing over at Wolfgang as he leaned against the post on the porch.

"For now." He raised an eyebrow in challenge, and my core warmed.

Ames dipped his hands over my hips and under the shirt that was barely covering me. "I approve of the new fashion choices," he purred in my ear. "I missed your honey taste of desire, little ghost."

I kissed him softly, but before I let myself get completely swept away, I broke free of his trance. "Onyx?" I reminded him of my earlier inquiry.

He let out an exhale and looked to Wolfgang, who only crossed his arms and shrugged. "Might as well tell her."

Ames held on to the hem of my shirt as I spun out of his hold. "Tell me what? Is he okay?"

Wolfgang took my hand. "Let's go sit in the backyard."

Ames wrapped an arm around my waist as I clutched my werewolf's hand. "Things in Belladonia are worse than they are here. The magic is not functioning properly. There are monsters here that shouldn't be. There are humans there that shouldn't be. Whatever happened during the blood ritual could have contributed to this and spit us all out years ahead of time and in different places. Onyx... he woke up on the throne. And his mother needed his help."

My heart constricted in my chest with a heavy fear and sadness. Onyx Hart, my vampire, my dragon, my love, was indeed the vampire king. And he'd... stayed for them.

"So he's not here?" I asked, my head immediately pounding

with tears that wanted to fall. Of course he should have stayed. Of course he belonged on a throne in the castle in the sky. But when I'd last seen him, I'd been dripping from his fangs, from his love, as we all joined together in intimacy and passion. How could such an act of love tear us apart, shredding the fabrics of time and space with it? And now we were apart again.

The guys and I rounded the corner and into Wolf's spacious backyard that was cradled by huge trees. In the center, a fire was raging. I rubbed my misty eyes and squinted at the blaze. "It's black," I said, stepping nearer. "How is it—"

A yelp squeezed from my ribs as something grabbed me from behind and lifted me. He spun me around and dipped me as if we were dancing, and both a laugh and a cry shook my shoulders as I wrapped my arms around my dark prince.

"Onyx," I cried, kissing his cold lips. I rubbed his perfect face, admiring his glowing green eyes, his down-turned black brows, and that widow's peak that was pure vampire. He smiled, fangs glinting.

"My Belladonna," he breathed, cupping my face and kissing me deeply. "Sorry I'm late. Once we arrived, we split up, and I stopped for marshmallows."

"Marshmallows? Really?" Wolf teased, grabbing Onyx in a hug.

The vampire shrugged. "My ancestry won't allow me to show up to a party empty-handed." His eyes turned sharp, and the teasing tone evaporated. "You bled." He rubbed his pale silver-ring adorned hands over Wolf's abdomen and sides. "Freshly healed. You must be sore as fuck. Ghoul and…" He examined the faint pink gashes. "No… How are diphylla in Ash Grove?"

Ames's jaw tensed. "We have a lot to figure out."

I slumped on a log, stretching my bare legs toward the fire. Looking up at my boys, I marveled at them, seeing them together, realizing we were all finally back in Ash Grove. There was much to sort through, and a lot of craziness to undo. But damn, it felt so good just having them all with me and being home.

"She tastes happy," Ames said to the guys.

"Smells happy, too," Wolfgang confirmed.

Onyx wrapped his arms around each of their shoulders. "Because I'm here. Obviously."

We chuckled, knowing we'd missed our hybrid's self-assured sense of humor. They joined me, and just their warmth and the crackle of the blaze lulled me into a calm I hadn't experienced in a long while. After a moment, I sat up from Ames's hold while Wolf rubbed my legs and Onyx's head rested in my lap. He gazed up at me with glowing emerald eyes, and I asked, "You left your mom?"

"Ah, she left me first."

Wolf snorted and shook his head. "Dark, bro."

"You left a kingdom that needed you for me? Onyx..." My heart twisted in guilt that he'd done exactly what I'd hoped he would. What did that say about me? That I couldn't forfeit one of my men to save a town or help lost souls? All because I wanted him near me at all times.

Onyx sat up and took my hand, lightly kissing my knuckle. "You're my empire, Blythe Pearl."

My throat constricted with emotion as I held his hand, feeling the touch of my men, absorbing their love in the faint moonlight of a broken Fenrir. "And you guys are mine. My kingdom, my kings, my home forever."

CHAPTER 14

Wolf

BAIT AND HOOK

You have to decide who you are and force the world to deal with you, not its idea of you.
James Baldwin

The farther I got from the night we arrived, the full moon, the night I shifted into an alpha, the more the toxic traits of the beast faded, or were at least easier to suppress. I wasn't jealous that Blythe was home alone with Onyx and Ghost. And not just that, I was actually thankful. She was probably glad to not be boarded in with no escape as well. Now that she was sleeping in and being looked after, I could assess the state of the pack. And what a sorry state it was.

Nephele and Carmine led me through the overgrown grass and showed me the land. The borders of poison daffodils, the narrow points of patrol, and the flimsy unit of barely of age lunas, stellas, and sols who performed the rounds. A running list formed in my mind of things I needed to do. Repair the chicken coop, build a barbed fence for the goats, take a running inventory of the dry pantry and the meat shed, scan the ghoul pit, mow the grass, fix the shingles of every fucking house… and then there was one other thing.

"And Laverna? It's in two and a half weeks," I inquired, crossing my arms in stress as I idly watched two pups collect rocks and throw them into a puddle.

Carmine answered, which grated on my nerves. "We weren't planning on celebrating. With the lunas and elders gone, the threats—"

"You seem to know me, but I don't know you," I cut in. "And you don't seem to know pack rules. Lunas are in charge. When I ask a question, the lunas or stellas speak first. You're an elder sol by default, not by earned rank. And regardless, you'll never be higher than a luna."

The man deflated a bit and rubbed his red beard. Good. Nephele answered. "I guess we can assemble some sort of Laverna if you'd like. It would go a long way in cheering up the people left."

"Put it together." I shrugged. "If you want to."

"You're the alpha. You make the rules," Nephele replied.

"Lunas are my alphas. Always. I'll help as I'm needed. We are equals in leadership, Nephele. I am no better than any other wolf here."

The luna hid a small smile and nodded. "Glad to hear you still abide by the ways of Fenrir pack. I'd like your permission to take your mate and some other lunas and introduce them to the festivities properly. It's not too late to plant certain species of buds. It would dwindle our security for the afternoon, but perhaps you and your friends can cover for us."

I nodded, lost in thought as the kids laughed, tossing in bigger rocks now.

The luna stood next to me and said in a low voice, "I've tried my best. I know it hasn't been enough. I know I'm not what Fenrir deserves. But I am committed to helping bring it back. I think you're an additional leader we need. If you want to take us on, that is."

"Where are the phantoms now?" I asked, not looking away

from the pups. The spring air was cold and sweet that morning, and they were barefoot in the mud.

The woman's white hair shook. "Everywhere. Nowhere. Go into town. You'll see what they've made of the place."

I cringed at the thought. Perhaps we'd leave Blythe to protect her from whatever was awaiting in downtown Ash Grove. The white wolf turned to leave, and I spoke, stopping her. "I'll take you on. All of you."

I guessed it was my destiny. It was what the elders and lunas before me would have wanted, what they all saw in me from the beginning somehow. I remembered being as young as the pups playing in the rainwater. My grandfather took me to the waterfall and let me steer the small engine on our boat as he napped under his bucket hat. "Wake me up if anything bad happens," he'd say as he tipped his brim over his brow and nodded off. I'd weave patterns through the lake, forgetting about the fishing lines trailing behind.

I wished I could wake him now. Because there were truly bad things happening. And this pack didn't seem to see that I was still just a pup, too. Or I felt like one, at least. I wasn't ready to be their leader, but I had to be. Somehow, I had to steer this boat to safety, like crazy Captain Vex and his crew. This was my crew, and this was my lightning storm to navigate. And that meant I needed to think outside the box and outside my pride. I sure as hell didn't want to do what I was about to do, but my old cellphone I'd grabbed on my way out that morning still worked and still only contained a few phone numbers.

My thumb flicked over the screen, and it rang once, twice, and then connection clicked. He never said hello. Devils were too cool for pleasantries, I guessed.

"You should get over here," I said into the void, pacing through the grass to hide my nervousness.

After what felt like ages of silence, he rumbled, "See you soon." And the line went dead.

Sending for Judas always felt like a mistake. He was closer with

Ghost, or perhaps he and Ghost understood each other better than he and I. I wasn't a creature of hell, as the guys were. My roots were earth and soil and my wolves. And I'd made mistakes with him before. But no one could know that. Because that was our goddamn *secret*.

SMELL WAS AN UNDERESTIMATED GIFT. Many wolf gifts were misread by the outside world. We didn't resent this fact. Instead, we leveraged it, counted on it. It was no mistake that through hundreds of thousands of years, wolves remained at the top of the food chain, even transcending the forests and embedding themselves in human lore worldwide. Wolves didn't need to flaunt strength or prowess. We embodied it and used it when the time came.

Being a wolf was much like being a man. A good man, that is. In recognizing our strength, we knew how to be soft, how to be caretakers of our mates, packs, and pups. To protect them in such a way that it unlocked their full potential. Because the thriving of the pack, the thriving of your mate, was a direct reflection of your power well used, your guardianship doing its job.

After I spoke with more of the community of Fenrir, helped make a couple dozen turkey sandwiches, and pulled about a hundred weeds from the herb garden, I made my way back to my cabin, feeling a bit more encouraged as to the state of the pack. The alpha beast inside me settled in my acceptance of taking Fenrir on as my own. However reluctant I initially felt, I knew I couldn't abandon them. There was much work to be done, but I could do it. I'd have to do it. Though I knew my alpha werewolf form was a lit stick of dynamite, waiting to explode again when the moon neared fullness... I would need to prepare the Halloween Boys, Blythe, and myself for that near future.

I rubbed the back of my neck and stretched my shoulders. The ache from getting my ass kicked last night still thrummed through me. But the aroma of combined passions instantly made my mouth water. Their intensity pooled over my front lawn as thick as Ghost's hell smoke. My girl was happy and satisfied, and that was a balm to my weary soul.

THAT NIGHT, I sat on my porch, staring out into the darkness. Occasionally scenting the patrol of wolves along the trees, sometimes hearing a screech of an owl or the scratching of a chicken. For how many creatures now haunted the woods and how few wolves there were, it was quiet. A little too quiet. Blythe was sleeping with Onyx, or whatever it was they did, while Ghost checked in on his graveyard. The wind rustled and stilled, announcing his presence, and he leaned against the post, arms crossed and brow furrowed.

"Bad, huh?" I asked, already knowing what his demeanor meant. You don't spend two hundred years with someone and not pick up on all their tells. It was a wonder we even needed words to talk to each other sometimes.

Ames let out an exhale. "Cat had help. Even so, a few damned escaped. Luckily, they didn't want to stick around. But that doesn't explain the ghouls and diphylla."

"Doesn't explain Fenrir or Belladonia either. I'm putting off a trip to town, but you know we have to check in on Ash Grove. They've asked for her. Twice now. Even in my alpha form, they weren't afraid. And they, or whoever's sent them, want Blythe."

Moments passed, and crickets sang and bounced in the grass. Being outside, the night air, the smell of the dirt, were the only things keeping me levelheaded. Outwardly, Ames looked so calm, but his fury was always so potent, so close to the surface of who he was. I wondered how he could stand it, how he could live with a volcano in his chest.

"I called Devil," Ames said after a moment. "He's been a little too scarce lately."

"Good idea," I responded, not mentioning that I'd made a call of my own. "Do you ever feel… leery about including him?"

"Every time."

"Why do we?"

The pale blue tint of Ghost that glowed beneath my friend's gaze caught mine in the night. "Better the devil you know."

CHAPTER 15

Blythe

LAZY HAZY CRAZY DAYS OF SUMMER

> …the June nights are long and warm; the roses flowering; and the garden full of lust and bees.
> *Virginia Woolf*

There was a lot to be learned about dating men. There was even more to be learned about dating monsters. Things were easy between us. Much easier than it had been before we left for Belladonia. Onyx seemed more at ease with himself, Ames had gotten past his possessiveness for the most part, and Wolfgang's alpha form hadn't made a reappearance. Though each of my Halloween Boys smiled with fondness and kissed me tenderly. I could sense from the way they'd exchange glances and the hardness of their shoulders that something was weighing on them. I wished they'd share with me or give me any sort of hint so I'd know what to ask.

But they were too good at being brick walls of secrets. To them, it was all in an effort to protect me, I was sure. But being left in the dark didn't put me at ease. To the contrary. It had me looking over my shoulder more often, worried when the other shoe was going to drop on our happy reunion. I knew what I needed, who I wanted, and I hoped she'd be waiting for me at

Magia Eclectics. Though the guys didn't seem as eager to venture into Ash Grove.

After they exchanged more of those morse-code, psychic-level glances of secrecy, Onyx put an arm around me and playfully pinched my ribs. They always had him say something they didn't want to say or didn't know how to say, I'd learned. And Onyx was good at it. But I was also getting smarter and picking up on their tricks. Someday, I'd best them at something. Someday, I'd see something coming and head them off. Then they'd respect me more. Then maybe they'd see me as more than the helpless damsel in need of constant saving.

"Belladonna, wouldn't you rather go to the graveyard with Ghost while Wolf and I check in on the town?"

"You don't want me coming. You can just say it," I cut off his charm, and Wolfgang chuckled.

Ames jeered. "You're losing your touch, Dragon."

Onyx gave him a belabored eye roll. "Okay, know-it-alls. But what happens when our darling kindhearted little poison flower walks into town and it's a burning pile of ghoul and diphylla ash? Is that what you'd rather me delicately warn her of?"

"I can handle it," I assured them. "You guys would be better off being straightforward with me. I'm *not* a delicate flower." I elbowed Onyx's side, and he nipped at my jaw, tickling me with his sharp fang. "I'm a deadly force of nature."

"You are," Ames agreed. "And ours to care for. We know how much Ash Grove means to you; we don't want your heart to break if it's in disarray. We've been gone a while, and a lot has likely changed, as it has everywhere else."

I looked over my shoulder at Wolf, who was stalking behind us with his hands in the pockets of his jeans. I directed my reply toward him, "Wolves adapt."

The corner of Wolfgang's mouth rose as I repeated what he'd said to me at the waterfall back to him.

"That's my luna," he whispered softly, and my heart melted into my boots.

Ash Grove was like a living entity, its own sort of ancient beast, and it had been through a lot. It would survive this, whatever this was, whatever awaited us. As we rounded the corner and down a grassy hill, something unexpected wafted through the air. I inhaled. "It smells like…" And then we heard music and the laughter of children. The guys looked to each other as I broke away, jogging forward, eager to see my home again. It was, remarkably, just as I remembered it. The old shops were still standing. Old men were walking around holding trays of taffy and sweets. And instead of orange and black decor, the historic buildings were adorned with reds and whites. A blue balloon floated past, and three kids holding ice cream cones squealed, brushing past me. I wandered through a small crowd, spotting Magia Eclectics over the music from the band playing in the center of the square.

Not only was Ash Grove not under siege by monsters, but it was… happy. Thriving even. The smell of popcorn and cotton candy was buttery sweet and made my mouth water as I walked by stalls selling pies and jewelry and wood carvings. A few old residents waved and smiled as I passed, as if it was just another day in Ash Grove, and I was just another friendly face passing them by on a normal, kooky, and magical day. The kind that had made me fall head over heels in love with this town. Apparently, that small-town charm wasn't isolated to October, at least not anymore.

Ames and Onyx stopped at my side. I thought I'd broken away from the group, but I should have known better. The look of bewilderment between them made me giggle like a maniac. I spun around and pointed at them both. "I don't know if I want to point out how *not* traumatizing this is or how nice it is for you guys to be the confused ones instead of me for once."

"She's been hanging out with you too much." Ames smirked, shoving his friend playfully.

Onyx put a hand to his chest. "Her wit is all her own. I merely aid her in her pursuit of darkness. You and Wolfgang need to, respectfully, fuck off."

Through my sides aching with laughter, Wolfgang appeared, parting the crowd with his broad stature. "Dad leaves for five minutes, and the kids are already fighting." He smiled, passing me a plastic cup.

I took a small sip. "Yum—"

"Where did you get beers?" Onyx asked in astonishment.

Wolf held up his palm. "You have to get a wristband."

Ames took the cup from my grip and gave it a taste. "IPAs are for pussies."

Wolf downed his drink before pulling me out of Ames's and Onyx's mutual touches for a warm hug. "That statement reeks strongly of toxic masculinity, my friend. You should consider therapy, Dr. Cove."

We all laughed heartily as banjos played, children twirled, and popcorn popped. It wasn't eerie Halloween briskness, but it was bright summer giddiness. And I had all my guys together, with all their ancient crankiness mixed with normal-dude charm. I felt as if I could pass out from exhilaration. The boys gathered around a street performer playing card games, and I tugged on Wolf's sleeve. He lowered his scruffy jaw so I could whisper in his ear, and the movement, the small moment of intimacy, sent a flutter of butterflies gliding on my breath.

"I'm going to pop into Magia and see if Yesenia is there. I'll be right back."

"Want me to come with you?"

On cue, my familiar landed on my shoulder. Wolfgang gave Raven's chest a gentle stroke with the back of his finger.

"We've got it. I'll only be a few minutes."

Before I could draw the attention of Ames or Onyx, I weaved through the people who'd gathered to watch the magic show and slipped into Magia Eclectics, jumping at the same ugly reaper Halloween decoration that laughed upon my entrance. We may have been gone for years, but that plastic thing would survive the apocalypse.

"One sec!" a youthful voice called from the back.

Taking in a lungful of Magia Eclectics air, I skipped over the oracle cards and pendulums and snatched up a lipstick. Peach would look nice for spring. Or maybe Wolf liked pink better…

"Well, well, well, if it's not Death on my very doorstep," the woman's voice crooned.

I turned, thinking I knew the voice, but found someone I didn't immediately recognize. From the curl of her long hair, the smokiness of her tone, and her undeniable magnetism that subtly let any human know she was not, in fact, just an ordinary mortal.

I asked, "Oh, do we know each other? Are you related to Yesenia and Marcelene? I'm actually looking for Yesenia."

The woman smiled and removed her glasses, polishing them on her purple skirt. "You won't find my granddaughter here, girl. Though I wish that weren't the case."

"Is she okay? Wait…"

Raven cawed and agitated his wings before the woman cackled a very witchlike laugh. The reaper buzzed as the door slammed shut, and I settled slightly as a broad, affirming hand comforted the small of my back. Joy—at the realization that the witches' wards could keep out evil like demons and vampires, but not the goodness of my werewolf—soothed me as my brain fought to put together the pieces of what I was witnessing.

"Marcelene," Wolfgang rumbled in greeting. "I see you're doing well."

I glanced up at him with wide *what the hell?* eyes, and he only raised his eyebrows, mirroring my perplexities.

"Quite well indeed, Wolfgang. It has been some time since the obscenity of the Halloween boys has graced these streets. As you can see, we are doing remarkable in your friends' absence."

Wolfgang growled low in his throat. "Perhaps if you'd spared a bit of magic that you used to make yourself appear young again on Fenrir, I could say the same about my community."

Marcelene pursed her red lips and leaned against the sales counter. "That is dreadful. I am sorry we couldn't do more. If the Moon Halo Coven could have only united instead of…" She shook her head. "Unfortunately, I do not have any spells to spare for the wolves. However, perhaps the phantoms could assist. They've been most helpful."

When the growl in my wolf's throat grew louder, I took his wrist with two hands and tugged him toward the door. "Where can I find Yesenia?" I pressed as I pulled against my boulder of a man.

"Goddess, if I know." Marcelene waved a sad and dismissive hand. "But go on and take the lipstick, child. No one buys it now without her here to sell them. The alpha wolves do prefer pink, by the way."

It dawned on me that the tube of makeup was still clutched in my palm as I shoved Wolf out the door. Despite the warm air that greeted us, a chill ran down my spine.

I opened my mouth to speak, but Wolf pulled me close, tucking me under his arm. "Something isn't right." He inhaled. "Dark magic smells like bitter smoke." Taking my hand firmly in his, like I was a toddler who could wriggle away and run at any moment, he led me through the stands and chatting townspeople.

"Where are the guys?" I asked, scanning the crowd.

"We can't talk openly here," he said lowly. "Everyone is listening. Fenrir," he said plainly, and I shut up.

When we were back in Wolf's old Ford Bronco, he exhaled. "We agreed that if there was an opportunity to gain insight into the phantoms' operations, we'd take it. Ames and Onyx did so, and I came to be with you in the magic shop."

A huff of annoyance rattled me as I crossed my legs and looked out the window. "Sounds like you guys have it all figured out, as usual."

"We're good at what we do. And what we do is keep people safe by eradicating threats. The chaos magicians have threatened Fenrir, and now Ash Grove."

"Do you think they have something to do with the ghouls?"

He didn't answer. Only the sound of rain splattering against the windshield and the rattling old engine filled the space between us in the muggy vintage car.

"Why do the ghouls want me?"

"It doesn't matter. They will all be dead soon."

We rolled to a stop, and my anger reached its boiling point. Opening the rusty car door, I stomped into the rain. The cold drench did nothing to extinguish my agitation. Another slam of a car door, and Wolfgang was in front of me, startling me with his speed. The downpour clung to his long curls and pasted his white shirt against every curve of his muscular chest, drawing my eyes to his body.

"Move," I ordered, trying to push past him.

"You think I'm going to let you go stomping off into the monster-filled forest alone? No fucking way." Steam rose off his shoulders from his warmth, taunting me as I shivered.

I shoved his rock-hard chest with all my might, and he didn't budge. Shoving again, I shouted over a burst of thunder. "I'm strong, too. I'm smart, too. But you'd never know it because you meathead men don't let me in the game. You don't fill me in on your stupid plans. If you had, I could have told you who the main phantom was. His name is Zyre, and he's a creepy asshole. But no, you all do this shit behind my back. I'm not your pet. I'm your partner, Wolf. Aren't I? Or am I just a random girlfriend? One of a million you've probably had."

Wolfgang shook his head and ran a hand through his wet hair. "You think just any girl could turn me into this—this fucking maniac?" He clutched his fists at his sides and growled, low and carnal, in his throat. "It took one time, Blythe. One time of being inside you, paired with one full moon, and we broke the fucking world. And you know what the ritual did? It spit us out together in the cemetery. You and me. It's always been you and me. Since the moment I laid eyes on you, I knew you were my luna, Blythe. My moon."

My breath came out in a cloud of cold air. Wolfgang stepped closer, wrapping his piping-hot arms around me. "But you're right. Keeping you in the dark isn't fair. You have to understand; we've been a team for hundreds of years. It's just been us and no one else. We're still learning the rules of this, and we're going to get it wrong sometimes."

I rested my forehead on his ribs before he tilted my chin to look at him. "But keep calling me out like that and see what happens. Because right now, I'm so fucking hard for you."

A smile broke my cold face. "You liked that?"

"Fucking loved it. A luna after my own heart."

"I like being your luna."

"Back to the car," he ordered with gentle authority as lightning splintered the sky. "Or I'm going to fuck you in the mud, and Onyx will never let me live that down."

Giddiness and giggles were never far from the surface of my humanity with Wolfgang. Where I was usually a quiet and contemplative sort of soul, Wolf was something so fresh and so pure. Though the glimpses of darkness and fierce canine prowess excited me, and all I wanted to do was coax that alpha out from his hiding spot. When we were back in the car, Wolf pulled me down the rain-slick leather bench seat.

Then his rough grip was on my hips, and I followed his guiding strength onto straddle his lap. Our kiss collided with a rumble of thunder as the storm beat against the metal of the car. I felt his fingertips ease under my shirt, his wide and hard-skinned hands taking up my whole middle as they found my breasts. A sigh mixed with desire and contentment left me as my mind toyed with how it was possible a man could inspire both. But Wolf did. Wolf was this creature of opposing facts. He was soft and compassionate, and at the same time, he was the most masculine force of nature I'd ever met. Wolfgang was a mountain. One I wanted to climb every day for the rest of my life. Scaling his heights and knowing his steady rock center would be there to hold me through every slip.

"I've never had sex in a car before," I admitted, grinding against the hard length straining behind his jeans. My delight in choosing to wear a cotton maxi-dress that day was apparent.

He smiled against my kiss, not letting me pull away. "Me neither," he replied, surprising me.

My giggle was muffled by his own chuckle as I reached between us to unbutton his pants. "You're so old, Wolfgang. How is that possible?" I teased.

"Never had you as my passenger-princess until now," he answered roughly. His breath hitched as I took his cock in both of my hands, leaning back to get a better look at him. My fingers didn't touch, didn't reach around his girth. I moved them up and down, exploring his sizable length.

"You're a god," I breathed in reverence.

He sucked my bottom lip between his teeth and growled, pushing against my hold, and my pussy ached to slip him inside me, but my hands were greedy to feel him, too. "Nowhere near a god, little one. Merely your humble servant for as long as you'll have me. I take no moment with you for granted."

"Wolfgang Jack," I whispered, the fog of our heat clouding the windows.

He took hold of himself and pulled me forward by my lower back. Then his hold took me by the hips and lifted me over him, before lowering me onto the head of his cock. His hand snaked between my thighs and moved the edge of my panties to the side, allowing him to slip in. I never knew leaving my panties on during sex could be so freaking hot. I let out a whimper, feeling every movement of his rounded head push against my small opening.

"If I were God"—his hot breath hit my ear as my forehead fell to his shoulder—"I'd trade all of creation just for the honor of holding you like this, Blythe. Feeling your tight walls, the nectar made just for me. What an honor to experience you like this, my luna."

Tears pricked my eyes. How could I love this man more and more every day? My love for him felt overflowing as it was. I wrapped my arms around his thick neck and kissed his lips softly and reverently as his hand tangled in my hair. Driving my hips down, I took him in halfway, and we both let out a sound of elation.

"I know I'm not as intense as Ghost or as charming as Onyx," he mumbled, breathless. "But I offer you all that I have, Blythe."

His eyes fluttered closed in bliss as I took him to the hilt, the stretch burning and aching passion through me. "You are *everything*, Wolf. Everything."

He took my hips again then and lifted me, then eased me back down until I cried out. Repeating the motion again and again, a dull ache built and built inside my core.

"Look at us together." He flicked his gaze between us, and I followed. My face heated at the sight of my pussy lips stretched pink around him. His long and wide shaft glistened, slick with our combined arousal. "I'm going to fill you up with me, and you're going to keep every drop inside. I want my cum in your womb, breeding you, owning you."

"Yes," was all I could utter. "That sounds so nice with you."

His fingers dug into the tender flesh of my thighs, then he pulled me deeper. My moan rivaled the storm as he hastened his movements with quick and mighty precision.

"You're so wet for me, little one," he growled as his sandpaper scruff brushed against my mouth, my cheeks, my ears, and down my neck. Wolfgang left no area of skin untasted; he ate me whole with every interaction, and I was addicted to being his meal.

The rain picked up, and I felt the coolness of the center of my panties drench with us. Every thrust tugged the middle strap against my clit, slipping harder and rougher against me with every plunge of my hips. The dull ache became insurmountable as I felt the scratch of Wolf's beard cut against my face as one hand held my hips and the other rose to wrap around my throat. He squeezed the sides firmly and growled his command, "Come for daddy wolf. Come on my cock, little one. Pour your juices down my knot."

The filthy order was my undoing, and I reverberated an explosion of pleasure along with the downpour. Wolfgang roared, vibrating the car and thrusting into me so deep as he pulled me by my throat down on top of his cock. His hot cum pooled inside me but couldn't flee, could only stay right where he wanted it, as his knot grew. My walls tensed and fluttered a pulsing orgasm around his growing bulge that lodged at my base.

"Deep breath," he commanded. "Easy, baby. You can take it," he directed me, so bittersweet against my jaw.

My head found the crook of his neck, my skin sticking to his with our perspiration as my tender pussy yearned against its affliction. The knot and cum filled me, pushing me into acceptance. I couldn't move, couldn't escape. I could only lie tangled in the arms of my predator. My hunting wolf had caught his prey, and I was at the hunter's mercy.

We stayed, riding out the aftershocks of our sex and the pelting of the storm. Wolf moved my hair out of my face and began tugging it behind me. I sat up slowly, feeling the pull between my legs where we still connected to each other. My anchor in the storm. "What are you doing?" I smiled, seeing him bite his lip in concentration.

"Braiding your hair back." He pulled an elastic band from around his wrist and tied the bottom of his creation. "There, that's better, hm?"

Shaking my head in disbelief at his tenderness, his beautiful heart, I kissed his lips softly. "Let's go home to Fenrir," I whispered between his lips.

His amber eyes lit with emotion as he nodded. "I'll take you home. Home with me, little one."

With his knot removed, we righted our clothing, and he fired up the car, holding me under his arm as I lay against his chest the whole drive home. The knot was more than sex, I realized in that moment. It was a symbol of our tying together. A knot, a binding, a promise. Wolfgang and I were forever tangled together in a knot too deep and twisted to ever be undone. And I was in awe of every curve and fray of our love.

"THE GUYS ARE BACK. I smell them. Though faintly because of the rain." He held my hand tight as we squished through the wet earth toward his cabin.

Relief washed over me when I stepped inside Wolf's warm cabin. A fire raged in the hearth as Ames sat with an ankle on his knee, reading a newspaper, and Onyx stood in a pink apron over the stove. "Take the scenic route, did we? In this weather? It took so long, one would think something unsavory was taking place in Wolfgang's truck," the vampire purred teasingly, kissing my cheek before returning to his concoction.

"Don't be rude," Ames said, looking up over his glasses. He patted his knee, and I happily obeyed, wrapping myself in his warm hold. "However, next sunny day, it's you, me, and my bike."

Excitement trilled through me, and I nodded eagerly. I'd missed motorcycle rides with my demon.

"How did it go with the phantoms?" I asked, watching Wolfgang inspect Onyx's cooking.

The hybrid whacked his friend's hand before passing me a bowl and a spoon. "A whole lot of nothing. Fucking clowns. They clearly have a monopoly on the town, keeping them thoroughly entertained and protected. But when we very politely inquired as to their master's whereabouts, or to speak with their chaos leader, they only replied in half-ass, cryptic riddles."

"Un-clever riddles at that," Ames added. "What do you think our next move should be, Wolf? Anything thrilling inside that old bat Marcelene's store? I know she isn't dead, unfortunately."

Wolf hummed, adding spices to the pot, despite Onyx's protests. "Blythe has some insights to share, I believe. Things we haven't thought of or have overlooked. So, go ahead, luna."

Onyx elbowed his friend playfully before resting his head on

Wolf's shoulder. "Alphas do so worship their lunas. Romantic nickname, man, I like it."

"Our Claimed is worth every bit of worship," Ames whispered, positioning his hand on the inside of my thigh.

My cheeks flushed at their collective praise. Individually, they were each anything and everything I could ever want. Together, they were unreal in their intensity.

The fire popped, and I stirred my soup while collecting my thoughts. I was nervous, not wanting to sound inexperienced, but this was what I wanted. I wanted to be included in the conversation, a part of the team, not just the helpless victim. "The lead phantom in charge is Zyre. He was there when I disappeared at the circus a few months ago. Wolf and Onyx have met him."

Ames's grip tightened on my thigh. "I knew something went down at that goddamn circus."

"Zyre," Onyx thankfully cut in, giving me a small wink as he did. Oh, my vampire. Always bailing me out of trouble with my demon. "I vaguely remember getting under his skin. I believe I set him on fire, but it's hard to remember him amongst many that fall under that category."

I bit my lip to hide my laugh. "And about Magia… Yesenia wasn't there, and it would seem she hasn't been for some time. Oh, and Marcelene is like, twenty again."

"This shit again." Ames rubbed his temple. "Always something with that coven of bats."

I sat up straight on his lap, setting my bowl on the end table. "And one more thing. Something I've been thinking about."

Wolfgang smiled, his pride emboldening me. "Go on. We're listening."

"I've been chased by something my whole life, it seems. My stepfather, my past, trauma, legions of demons, and now these monsters in the woods. They can't seem to see me, which is good, but hiding can't be my only defense. I'm still learning what I'm capable of as a reaper, but I don't want to rely on that. You guys don't rely on just your abilities, and I shouldn't either."

"What are you asking?" Ames inquired, rubbing my leg in a distracting pattern.

I couldn't believe what I was about to ask, but it was time. I was tired of running, tired of being a victim of the violence stalking me. It was time. "I want to learn to fight. No, I want to know how to kill. Just like you guys."

CHAPTER 16

Ghost

OLD DOG, NEW TRICKS

> I thought I would be understood without words.
> *Vincent Van Gogh*

Over one hundred ghouls roamed the forest of Ash Grove. More than I'd ever encountered. Tracking the diphylla was like counting dead leaves, and my hell smoke could hardly get a read on them since they were crafted and deformed versions of vampires. But the situation wasn't good. The wolves were disorganized. Ash Grove was a pawn in some circus freak's game, and a few damned had escaped the cemetery already. In the midst of this calamity, Wolf's alpha had activated, which was an asset in battle, yet a liability when it came to Blythe's safety and our ability to chart our next move. We'd been gone for years, but how?

And something greater hunted my Claimed. Though somehow, despite all this, we were warm in Fenrir as rain pelted the tin roof of Wolf's modest cabin. It all felt right as long as she was in my arms and safe. The urge to lock her up was still there, but I'd leaned into the security and love that the Halloween Boys offered her. I took delight in seeing her blossom alongside spring's tulips.

The taste of fear on my tongue was duller and duller, even

when threats inched in around us. My little ghost was getting braver, because of us, but mostly because of her. Because she was strong, and she'd been through hell. But instead of that hell burning her alive, she'd turned it to strength. With or without the reaper abilities that lurked beneath her surface, Blythe was powerful, and I was more in love with her with every passing moment.

Though the thought of her fighting, taking part in the gore of battle, sent resistance and worry pulsing through me. That was my job, our job. To fight for her, to offer her the blood of her enemies in gold goblets for her pleasure. But I couldn't say no if she wanted to procure that offering for herself. I couldn't deny her knowing how to defend herself. It could only be an asset, another weapon in her arsenal. And she just happened to be mated to the strongest men on the planet. We could teach her. She could learn from an archdemon, a vampire-dragon, and a werewolf.

In the stillness, I looked up, becoming aware that everyone was staring at me. "I'm fine with that. Though it's not up to me; it's up to her. We should train her individually, and then together. And with some work, I believe she'll have the skills she needs to kill."

Onyx clutched his heart, looking comical still wearing Wolf's floral apron. "My little demon is growing up and forfeiting some of his possessive inclinations. I'm so proud."

Picking up a pillow, I chucked it at him as Blythe laughed. "It's to her benefit."

Wolf tugged off his damp T-shirt, commanding all of our attention with his perfect physique. "Plus, imagine how hot she'll be fighting."

Onyx hummed. "Slitting throats and bleeding monsters dry."

"You guys are deranged," she teased, tensing her knees together as honey invaded my mouth.

Wolf prowled closer and dropped to kneel, putting his hands on either side of the couch. "Individually and then together, you say? Maybe we could skip ahead a little bit?"

My kiss found the crook of her neck as I murmured my agreement. "Working as a team takes a lot of practice." I tugged at her dress, peeling it off, the fresh powdery scent of her hair only teasing me further. "Her panties are wet, too," I mentioned to Wolf, rolling them down her full hips.

"I wonder what else is wet for us," he growled, no doubt smelling her honeyed arousal as intensely as I was as it pooled in my mouth.

Onyx removed his ridiculous apron and crossed his arms, leaning against the butcher block counter. His eyes glowed in rapt focus as they roamed her lush and naked form. She leaned back into me, sighing as I twirled her little pink nipples between my thumbs and forefingers. Wolfgang let out a low vibration from his throat as he picked up her leg and rested her ankle on his shoulder. "This time, no one's making me stop until I've had my fill." He glanced over his shoulder at Onyx, who only shrugged. "No promises, big guy. I'm awfully thirsty."

Blythe whimpered, squirming on my lap as my erection pressed into her ass. "You guys are going to kill me."

Wolf kissed the inside of her knee. "Careful who you ask for lessons. We're easily distracted and morally corrupt teachers, my sweet luna." She tried to pull her leg away as he moved up her thigh with kisses and small bites, but I held her hip in place.

"His beard tickles," she said, breathless when I wouldn't let her move.

"Ah, but you're going to be a good girl and lie nice and still on me while Wolfgang worships your delicious little cunt, aren't you?"

With a nod, she watched as he looked up at her with a devilish smile. "Get comfortable, Ames. I'm going to take my time."

And that he did. Pushing her toward climax, only to pull away. He'd have her moaning and writhing, and instead of letting her own her bliss, he'd remove a finger and slow his pace, starting the sampling over again.

"Fuck," Onyx complained, pulling out his cock and stroking himself as he watched. "This is the most mouthwatering torture."

"Yes, torture," Blythe complained, finding my mouth for a dazed kiss.

I chuckled into my Claimed's lips, enjoying the feel of her thick ass on my lap and her breasts under my palms. "Perhaps our werewolf friend needs a taste of his own torment?"

Onyx smirked. "With delight." He wrapped Wolf's ponytail around his wrist twice and pulled him upright. "If you're going to be a gluttonous, selfish prick, you'll at least share what of her is on your lips. Give me a taste of both of you."

Wolf's short, cropped beard was glistening with Blythe's eros, and I was nearing my own limit for how much longer I could wait before being inside her. Dragon pulled Wolfgang's face to his, and their kiss was fervent with need. Suddenly, Blythe gasped as Onyx moved and blood dripped down his chin, mixing in the werewolf's facial hair. Our bloodthirsty friend sucked Wolf's lip, and he groaned, gripping the back of Onyx's neck and reaching down to palm his cock. "Fuck me while I finish devouring our mate," Wolf demanded, dropping his pants and returning to his position between Blythe's legs.

"God, it never gets old watching you guys do that," she whimpered as his blood-stained lips made contact with her aching center again. He groaned in pleasure, licking her, as Onyx wiped the remaining blood from his chin and swiped it across the target he'd laid on Wolf.

My own agony was bursting at the seams of my jeans, and I reached between Blythe's soaked flesh and me and pulled it out, positioning it under her. Wolf spread her legs farther, and I yanked her hips back. She yelped as we moved her into the position we wanted. "I have to have my cock inside you," I ground out into her ear as she moaned, feeling me slip into her from behind.

Onyx must have done the same, because Wolf paused for a moment, grunting as the vampire exhaled, pushing into his lover. "Look at you and Blythe, taking cock so well, as always."

She moaned while Wolf dipped again as Onyx pummeled in and out. I did the same, thrusting upward, deeper and deeper inside. Her arousal pooled alongside the werewolf's saliva, and I felt swipes of his tongue while he circled her clit, pressing in and sucking with reverence and awe.

I reached around, unable to control myself, and toyed with her pussy alongside him, careful not to get in the way of his meal. Getting in the way of a wolf's meal was always a bad idea, and I valued my human digits. And then that sound that I loved so dearly. My Claimed's scream, guttural and laced with desire. She bucked and whimpered as Onyx continued his thrusts. My own release exploded, and Wolf never stopped his assault, drinking in her orgasm along with the black seed of mine that wept from her opening.

Onyx swore, taking in the sight of us, and buried himself to the hilt, coming with want and with love during our collective passion. Blythe pushed against his face, sore and sated, but the werewolf didn't stop. "I'm not done," he growled. "Again," he commanded.

Blythe looked to me, and I chuckled, still firmly lodged inside her tight pussy. "I'm not going to save you from him, little ghost. I much agree, actually. I think you can come again for us."

"But he's so mean," she half laughed as Wolf sat up with a smirk.

"Let's give the crybaby a turn, then—and me a turn on him." Wolf and Onyx switched places, and the vampire happily obliged. But before he lowered, he glinted a fang. "I can't promise I'll be much nicer, though, Belladonna. Like I said, I'm terribly thirsty."

She cried out as he moved with a flash of speed. I'd pulled out just in time, giving him ample room to sink his fangs into the swollen lips of her sex. Her moan rattled, and tears streaked her face as she gasped in pleasure at the vampire's ravenous feeding. Her nails dug into my forearms as she held on through the racks of sensation. His bite was sending jolts of release through her gorgeous body, and he was greedily drinking her blood, her essence, and her orgasm within the same feed. I'd have to congratulate him later for achieving such a feat. But his own release was vibrating through him, sending him into a frenzy, as Wolfgang mounted him, thrusting with the hard and fast force the two loved together.

They were rough and carnal, and their grunts and pants, mixed with Blythe's moans of frenzy had my cock hard and dripping black again. My previous and overzealous, arrogant assessment of our inevitable polyamory had long since faded and sunk beneath the oars of Captain Vex's ship. This was right. This was us. And I could now picture no other way of being with her, offering her all of this, any time she required it.

As the night's activities waned from blazing to smoldering coals, we tangled in each other, wrapping Blythe in Wolf's furs and lying positioned around her, all of us touching her in some way. Our collective euphoria was enough to destroy worlds, but I wouldn't forfeit it, even to save the world. This was all I needed. To hell with the rest.

CHAPTER 17

Wolf

LITTLE FOX

> I have love in me the likes of which you can scarcely imagine and rage the likes of which you would not believe. If I cannot satisfy the one, I will indulge the other.
>
> *Mary Shelley, Frankenstein*

Blythe's scream pulled me from my deep sleep. It happened again. I'd let my guard down. We'd all stayed up into the late hours, fucking, kissing, taking each other. My agitation had cooled, and I'd slept in a pile with my family, my pack. My mate and my boys. And something had chosen that time to attack. I leapt from the floor and was by her side in a moment, and so were Ames and Onyx, where she was crying into Onyx's chest. He looked at me with furious green eyes as Ames let out a shout of rage and frustration. It took me a moment to take in the information. First I scanned her from head to toe. No marks, no blood. She was safe and whole and here.

And then I smelled it.

Death and the rotting flesh of animals. When I looked around, a few wolves looked on with horror at the misty morning fog that was dotted with patches of red fur. Fox fur.

The dead foxes were laid and arranged in a path leading to my house and scattered along the porch. Kneeling, I placed a hand on the cold pelt as a beady, vacant eye stared up at me.

"I'm sorry, friend," I said to the animal. The animal I didn't save... again.

Pushing on its corpse, I found what I knew I would. "Drained of blood—"

"I'll take Blythe inside," Onyx interrupted, giving me a look that told me not to say too much, not to scare her further.

Blythe straightened and dried her eyes. "No, I'm not going anywhere. You're not leaving me out of this. They want me, don't they? This is the same thing that happened in October, Yesenia told me months ago. I know you guys tried to hide it from me."

Horror struck me at her quick assessment. So much had happened. I'd assumed that attack had been dealt with. The ghoul who'd littered the churchyard with foxes matching Blythe's Hallows Fest costume was suffering for all of eternity for his crimes. But then... here was the same attack again. And it had happened inside the walls of Fenrir, with the Halloween Boys sleeping on the other side of a thin wall.

Ignoring Ghost's raging fit, which didn't fucking help anything, I pointed to a young man. Apollo, I believed his name was. "Find the pups first and make sure they're accounted for. Then get me a head count on every resident here, got it?"

"Yes, sir," he agreed, shifting into a gray wolf and running off.

"Ghost, get rid of these," I ordered, sadness cracking my tone at my obvious and utter failure. As Ghost's hell smoke covered the ground and the lifeless orange bodies, they sank into the soil. It was a burial fit for nobody, least of all a creature as majestic as the red fox.

I held my head. "I should have set up a patrol the moment I got here. I've guarded Blythe on the porch every night since we came, except last night." Fuck. I wanted to punch something, kill something.

"They've been watching us closely, then," Onyx said lowly.

"They've been watching us since Halloween. Maybe even before. And they want Blythe. They remember her costume. They want us to know that."

Ghost stomped up my stairs, his demon form terrifying in the blue light of dawn. "I'm going into the forest and killing every single fucking ghoul and diphylla, and I'm not coming back until they're all beneath the ground in my graveyard."

Reckless and improbable as it was, I wasn't going to stop him. But unfortunately, I couldn't join. "I need to address Fenrir. From now on, one of us is on patrol at all times, one of us is with Blythe at all times."

"I've got her," Onyx assured.

Blythe wiggled out of his hold. "I'm meeting with Nephele today, and it's lunas only."

Before Onyx could argue, I nodded. "She's safe with the lunas."

As I made to step off the deck, two small hands palmed my bicep. I turned, and Blythe hugged me tight. "It's not your fault," she whispered.

She was wrong, though. It was my fault.

But I would fix it. I would murder whomever and whatever was responsible for the threat against Fenrir and my mate. And I'd be doing it soon.

CARMINE PACED along the main entrance to the woods, huffing with an arched copper back. It was my first time seeing the sol's wolf form, and it was impressive. I could feel his disappointment as I approached. "Patrol last night was fine. It was raining, though, and I must have missed a scent trail."

"It was raining," I thought out loud. "But since when are ghouls smart?"

"Fucking never. But these ghouls and those bat creatures aren't like any I've encountered. I smell no fear on them. No fear of wolves? You can see why we've been confounded. And they just waltzed into Fenrir undetected, leaving carcasses to taunt us."

I rubbed my chin as Apollo skittered to a stop, kicking up rocks as he did. Typical teenage sol. Too much energy; not enough sense. "Whole pack's accounted for, Wolfgang, sir."

"I'm adding you to the patrol. And your friends. Anyone not a pup is acting as patrol. We're doubling our security protocols, and when you're not on watch duty, I want you pulling weeds. Send the others to me for their tasks. There's a lot to be done around here."

"That's a lot of work for a young one," Carmine challenged. "Seems like a lot of work for the women, too."

My jaw tensed. "Seems like there's a lot that needs fixing in Fenrir. Mend the chicken coop when you're off watch. Your job as a sol in this pack is in service of the lunas, same as me, so watch your fucking attitude. As far as I'm concerned, this breech is on you, Carmine. It wouldn't have happened if the lunas were guarding in your place."

He huffed in annoyance and continued pacing.

Before I was out of earshot, I asked him, "Where's the lead phantom usually stationed?"

"I don't know. He's always come to us. But I'd guess he's with the circus. They're just outside the town line of Ash Grove. Hard to smell, though."

Like I'd suspected, it looked like I'd be getting another ticket to the circus.

CHAPTER 18

Blythe

APPLES FOR TREES

You were wild once. Don't let them tame you.
Isadora Duncan

I'd anticipated a commotion of emotions and disorganization when I met with Nephele and the lunas of Fenrir. Maybe because that's how I was feeling with seeing my boys' ire this morning, knowing something was after me, and feeling Wolfgang's sadness over the deteriorating state of his pack's safety. But the white wolf was calm and serene as she sat by the rushing creek. The sun glinting off her fur made her look like a beacon of light. She shifted, and the other women looked to her as I leaned by a poplar tree.

"Despite everything, we're moving forward with celebrating Laverna. We won't let our culture die at the hands of darkness. That simply isn't who we are as wolves." The lunas agreed, each of them fiercely beautiful and strong. They probably didn't cower and cry at the sight of the dead foxes like I did. Instead, they gathered together, and they moved forward. "The first alpha sol in centuries has taken a mate, and she is here. This is our first Laverna with her and with him, so let's make it special, shall we?"

Nephele smiled at me warmly and took my hand, placing

something round in my palm. "Your bulb," she explained. "Ironically, the only thing I could find that would bloom quick enough for Laverna is a moon flower. It's a special plant. You're a rare luna to have it, and to have the love of our alpha as well."

My cheeks reddened. "I'm not a luna," I corrected her. "I'm actually… I'm a reaper. I'm Death." For some reason, I felt comfortable sharing that with her and the others in the group. Fenrir felt safe, the wolves felt safe, no matter what was going on around us.

"Do you want to be a luna wolf?" It was a strange question, but I answered honestly.

"I do, actually. You're all so strong. You command the men around you with such poise. You fight and hold your own. Those are all things I envy and want to learn. I have my own pack, so to speak, with the Halloween Boys, and so often they see me as this weakling. I'm learning to fight, but I think what I need to learn goes beyond that."

Nephele nodded. "You're wise, Blythe. And being a wolf, being a luna, comes from inside." She patted her muscular chest. "We accept all peoples at Fenrir. You're a wolf if you want to be one."

"I like that." I rubbed at the dirt on the bulb. "So what do I do with this?"

Two other girls with long multicolored braids joined us. "I'm Juno and this is Maia. Your first Laverna, how exciting." She clapped. "You know that this is our fertility celebration, yes?"

"Wolf's mentioned that before, yes. But what do the flowers have to do with it?"

The two lunas giggled while Nephele grinned on. "Lunas or stellas plant their seeds in the wintertime, generally. Planting as many as they like as far or as near as they like. When the moon is full on Laverna, we wait around a bonfire for our mates to find our blooms. The smell of the flowers will magically call to them, and they'll find the ones their mate planted. When they return, we…"

"Fuck like rabbits," Juno interjected, eliciting a gentle wave of laughter around us.

"I was going to say celebrate, but sure, that's part of it. Then we all come together and dance and feast around the fire on the full moon of spring. Truly, it is a joyous thing to take part in. Wolves look forward to it every year."

Juno looked me up and down. "Though we haven't had an alpha sol in, like, a million years. They're… extreme. How will she survive him?"

Nephele furrowed her brow in concern. "It's true that typically an alpha's mate is wolven, though that's not always the case. Even in his alpha form, he will protect her. At least, I hope so." Well, that wasn't very reassuring. The white wolf squeezed my shoulder. "Ready to plant?"

Raven glided above me as I spent the afternoon wandering the woods with the lunas, sticking to the spots where the yellow daffodils bloomed. They explained how the creatures in the woods stayed away from the flowers, hating the scent and being burned by the petals, so we were safe from attack. Apparently, my time in Fenrir had lifted the yellow flowers' curse on me, or at least I'd assumed as much, when they didn't affect me the way they had when I'd first come here. My sense of smell was becoming keener, too.

With each new shrub or trail the lunas would point out, I'd catch the faintest buzz of its unique aroma. Maybe there was a bit of luna in me after all. *Trust your nose*, they'd say. *Your eyes and ears will play tricks on you, but smell never lies.*

I broke away from the pack for a moment, finding a spot in the woods surrounded by smooth black stones. It was perfect for planting my bulbs. Dirt lodging under my nails felt wonderful as I dug at the earth. After planting my little bulb, I stood, and my heart jumped at what I heard. The whistling was back. I looked around for the source, when they made a clicking sound above me.

"When are you going on your journey? You know they're waiting for you." The voice of the little wooden creature sounded from a branch on a pine tree.

"Everything all right?" Juno asked, walking over silently, her wolfish skills hidden in plain sight.

I pointed to the tree. "I'm fine. It's just I think the tree, or a tree spirit, is messing with me."

She giggled. "They do that. I heard a story as a pup, of a wolf who fell in love with the voice of a mountain. They say she abandoned everything to live in its caves just to hear the mountain speak."

"That's lovely. And sad," I replied, squinting through the pines and coming up short. The little spirit was gone.

"It says I'm going somewhere. A journey. And something about a veil? They're confusing to speak with."

Juno didn't seem alarmed as she fished two green apples out of her pack and handed one to me. "If a forest spirit has latched on to you, it's best to listen. They'll look after you. But it's wise to bring them an offering. Trees like fruit and berries, things like that. Might warm them up to explaining things in a more human way."

"Thanks for the tip," I said, following her back to the main group.

A howl tore through the forest, and the lunas glanced at each other. I'd come to know my werewolf's sound, so I asked, "What did he say?"

Nephele took a bite of beef jerky and offered me a piece. "Wolfgang wants us to double our defensive patrol. Basically, security for Fenrir."

"Sounds like he's drafting the teens in as well. Lunas, sols, stellas, everyone. I'll set up camp in the middle of the commune," Juno supplied.

The mood was tense on the hike back, and when I arrived, Onyx was waiting for me. He bowed with his usual charisma and offered me his hand. "Shall I escort the lady back to her chambers?"

I glanced over my shoulder as Nephele ordered the lunas about. Each received a duty and eagerly took it on. Some went to help with food, others to set up camp and arrange patrol. Taking

Onyx's marble pale hand, I noticed the soil still under my nails and the taste of smoke from the dried meat still heavy in my mouth as Juno and Maia tossed logs in a pile to build a fire. They'd be up all night looking after the pack, looking after me, defending me from terrors that chased me here. Fenrir was collateral damage, and in part, it was my doing. But even more than that, I knew I couldn't leave them out here to do the work alone. I couldn't hide inside while Wolf carried the weight of the pack on his shoulders.

Onyx kissed my knuckles. "Wolfgang's cooking for the pack tonight. Hope you like rabbit. If not, I've procured your favorite chips and salsa back at the cabin."

I pulled my hand from his. "I'm not going. I'm staying here with the lunas."

He raised a dark eyebrow. "That's noble, truly, Belladonna. But I think the wolves have it under control."

"And I'm going to help."

"No offense, my love, but you're the bait. I'm not sure how helpful the bunny could be in a den of wolves."

His comment stung, though I knew he didn't mean for it to. The sentiment was accurate, and also not accurate at the same time. I wasn't a bunny. I refused to *stay* a bunny, at least.

As usual, at the first hint of trouble, Wolfgang appeared, still drying his hands on a dish towel. "What's going on? Do you need something?"

"She thinks she's camping out here and patrolling with the lunas," Onyx informed him. "I told her no, but she's being stubborn."

"You didn't just tell me no." I poked at his chest, and he raised his eyebrows in amusement. "You called me a bunny, and I am *not* a helpless little critter."

The corner of Wolfgang's mouth curved. "Then what are you?"

I looked between them before taking a step back. Wolf stopped Onyx from following after me. "I'm a luna, a wolf. And I'm going to go help the others tonight. You guys will manage without me."

I made it all of ten yards before Wolf tugged on my wrist and spun me around. "You're not talking me out of it. I'm serious—" But before I could finish my thought, his lips crashed into mine. His rough palms smelled like rosemary as they cupped my jaw, and his tongue darted into my mouth.

When he stopped, leaving me breathless, he whispered, "I didn't think I could feel for anyone as deeply as I do for you. And I just fell so much more in love with you back there. You are my luna and my moon, Blythe Pearl."

"Your pack is my pack, Wolfgang." He pulled me closer this time, pressing my body to his, letting me feel the hard length growing between us. I reluctantly broke our kiss and bit my lip. "If this is some sort of reverse psychology trick to get me to come back with you so we can make out… it's kind of working."

Wolfgang laughed in that deep and soul-warming way of his before kissing my forehead. "I'm going to serve dinner. I'll see you on your first patrol, but I'm putting you with Nephele. Don't go trying to go alpha crazy right off the bat. Ghost's got you covered on that aspect."

I groaned. "Has he really been out killing things all day?"

"All day," Wolf confirmed. "Let's hope he's tired when I tell him what you're up to. For both of our sakes. Because he'll either be furiously angry or insanely turned on. Either way, your whereabouts are spoken for tonight. I'll make sure he knows that."

"Thank you, Wolf," I said, rising onto my tiptoes and kissing his cheek. I hoped he knew why I was thanking him. *Thank you for believing in me. Thank you for giving me the space to grow. Thank you for being the sunshine to my bulb in the dirt...* He smiled, like he knew, before returning to his work. And leaving me to begin mine.

NEPHELE PACED at the forest entrance. It was a pathway into spooky, forbidden darkness. One I was drawn to, despite the horrors that scratched and howled just beyond Fenrir's borders. "Wolves are opportunistic hunters," she explained. "We utilize our unique skills and take down our enemies based on their weaknesses, or even their lapses in judgment during battle. We're always looking for the most energy-effective kill."

"I'm not sure I have any skills *or* killer instincts." I shifted my weight, indeed feeling like a weak little bunny surrounded by fearsome predators. Onyx was right.

The women were lit with orange firelight as they listened. Nephele's smile of pride when I joined her, telling her I was staying to help, warmed me almost as much as Wolf's did.

Juno replied, "Everyone has their strengths and weaknesses. It's about awareness and accountability. How do you think us wolven rose above the alpha sols, asserting our leadership as equal or above their own? Not all packs used to operate like Fenrir's, but over time, it became apparent the lunas' authority was superior for a pack's survival."

Maia nodded, tossing a stick into the fire. "Men are far too emotional to lead. No offense to your mates, Blythe, but they'd choose you over their pack any day."

I giggled. "You're not wrong."

Maia brushed dirt off her pants. "I think you're good at letting people underestimate you, Blythe. Letting people assume your shyness is weakness. That's a strength, a sneaky one. Very wolvenlike. But don't let your pack of boys forget that you're in charge."

Nephele agreed. "Wise words, lunas. And Blythe does seem to have many hidden gifts." She squeezed my shoulder. "And your scent is nearly untraceable. Humans and immortals alike don't know what you are, can't sense you, and don't see you coming. Use that to your advantage, but don't believe them. Play your own game."

They were right, but I'd never pieced it together so succinctly. "I've been captured before. A few times, actually. And I never know what to do. I freeze when we've been under attack, forcing the guys to protect me."

Juno paced the tree line. "It *would* suck not to have claws and teeth."

Maia added, "But you have claws and teeth of your own. You just have to find what they are. The vampire was telling us earlier that you've freed spirits, fought baphomets, and killed a hoard of diphylla without barely lifting a finger. Sounds like teeth to me."

"Well, when you say it like that, it sounds impressive, but I have no idea how I did it."

Nephele put a hand on my shoulder. "First, you need to believe that you can. Second, you should find an elder, whatever that is for you. Elders are vital to the strength and training of the pack. Someone wiser, further on their journey, can help unlock your gifts. In the meantime, focus on being undetectable, and perhaps practice the killing without lifting a finger thing on ghouls, should they attack again."

We stationed at the base of a mossy tree, and I stared into the dark of the woods, the crickets chirping dulling out my thoughts. At first, I was afraid a ghoul or monster was lurking, waiting to jump out at me. Then I hoped one would so I'd have something to do.

Something tugged at a lock of my hair, and I startled, relieved to see a flash of my vampire prince.

"Oh, so Ghost and Wolfgang can stalk you, but I can't?" he teased softly, taking a seat next to me and staring into the woods. "And I didn't mean to hurt your feelings earlier. You're right. You're not a bunny."

I huffed a small laugh. "I forgive you." He wrapped an arm around my shoulders, nestling me into the crook of his fiery dragon warmth.

"You know, the witches say you're not supposed to stare into the woods like this. Something might stare back." He half grinned, flaunting a sharp fang.

"How are you? Like, really?" I asked, fidgeting with the silver ring on his forefinger. "We haven't gotten to talk much since Belladonia. You left that grand city and your mom for me? Gave up being king? That can't be true, Onyx."

I'd been so immersed in Wolf's world, I'd neglected to ask after my hybrid prince. He'd been through a lot and yet still put on his comfortable guise of magnetism. It was an effort to look past it and into who I knew he truly was beneath all the irreverence and games.

"Turns out gold crowns majorly clash with my wardrobe."

"Be serious."

"I am. You think it's hard for me to be selfish? You don't know me very well then, my dear. Or perhaps you see me through the lens of love."

"How did you guys get back?"

He put a hand on my inner knee as something twitched and broke a branch in the forest beyond. His glowing green eyes noted the movement and must have deemed it nothing before he continued. "Flew here as the dragon. He loved it; Ames hated it. It was a great time stretching the old wings."

"You could go back, you know. Check on your mom," I eased gently.

"I do worry about her. But right now, my focus is you and Wolf and getting this sorted out. Ash Grove is my first home. It's not as grand as a gothic castle in the sky, but it's my home. And you guys are my family first. Once this is put right, we'll see. But leaving you all isn't on the table, if that's what you're urging. I'm not leaving you. Ever."

It shouldn't have pacified a worried part of me, but it did. He wasn't the greedy one. I was. After a little while, drowsiness pulled at my eyelids. I was already shirking my guard duty.

Onyx tapped a slow rhythm on my shoulder. "I went back to my house to grab you some clothes and maybe a guitar or two."

I hummed. That sounded nice.

"But… it wasn't there."

I blinked, waking up. "Someone stole your stuff?"

"No," he assured, still casually tapping my arm. Playing a melody in his head, no doubt. "They burned it down."

CHAPTER 19

Onyx

SEX IN ASHES

Have you ever seen hell in someone's eyes and loved
it anyway?
Maram Rimawi

My belladonna had taken the news harder than I did
when I discovered it. I kicked through the ash pile,
kneeling to pick up a splintered box. The latch was
black with soot, but the contents were untouched. Thumbing the
locket, I picked up the curl of hair tied with green ribbon. Lifting it
to my nose, I inhaled. "What a state, huh, Minnie?"

She would have loved Blythe. My first love would have agreed
that my final love was far better suited for me than she was. But I'd
always love her, and knowing my father had a hand in her death
made rage simmer in my chest. I didn't care that my cottage was
gone. In fact, I'd expected something like it to happen eventually.
You don't live as long as I had and mingle with immortals and not
make a hefty number of enemies. Enemies that wouldn't fucking
die. Or worse, *couldn't* fucking die.

But my time back in Fenrir, as much as it went against my
every arrogant and selfish bone, would not be about me. This was
about Wolfgang and his wolf pack. And it was about Blythe

finding her footing again, in the way they'd both helped me find mine. My loves. They certainly complemented each other well, as if they were tailored to fit my every broken part. And in Wolfgang's newfound alpha form and rapt attention on my belladonna, his lust lit me within and kindled like a fire of passion, love, and trust. I loved them. I loved them together.

Though somehow, something a little different, something I hadn't noticed in maybe a decade, was happening. Ghost's stare was catching me more often than not. I'd wanted to bring him with me here today, but declined to bother him in his graveyard. But part of me wanted him with me now, to feel his touch, his solid and stern decrement that would calm my torrent of emotional melodrama.

An engine I recognized cut in the distance, and something paced through the forest, clamoring as it went. My heart swelled as I turned and met a piercing blue stare.

"Didn't know you'd be here," Ames gruffed, dropping a bundle of plywood to the ground.

I turned on my typical mask of charm, still clutching my memory box. "What's with the wood, or are you just happy to see me?"

Ames was a quiet man. Brooding. Always seemingly lost in his own darkness. I could see him and Blythe relating to each other in that way. My two melancholy darlings. He climbed the mountain of nothing and stood next to me, kicking a sharp spike from the debris. "Found it like this shortly after we returned to Ash Grove, though I think it best not to tell Wolfgang or Blythe. I'd rather not upset them right now." He ran a hand through his black hair. "I salvaged a few of your things already. Some leather jackets, a harmonica, some photographs. They're in my church for now."

I raised my eyebrows. "That was kind of you. But why are you here now?"

He reached into his pocket and pulled out a square bottle of cinnamon whiskey. "I'm rebuilding it for you."

"What?" I unscrewed the lid and slumped into a messy pile of burnt curtains. "Rebuilding my house?"

"Yeah, I am. Our house. We'll all live here as a proper family when I'm done."

I chuckled darkly, letting the alcohol burn the emotion from my throat. "They'll appreciate that."

"Do you appreciate it?" His silvery and intense gaze made me glad I was sitting, because he surely would have made me weak in the knees.

"What do I matter?" I passed him the bottle as he sat next to me and watched his full lips curve as he took a sip.

He exhaled, looking out over the overgrown farm I'd tended futilely for hundreds of years, all while my father's castle floated in some sky realm above me. While he looked down on me, killed my fiancée, drove my mother mad.

"You've always mattered to me, Onyx. More than you'll ever know." Ames's rough voice shook me from my self-pity and replaced those thoughts with more… colorful ones. "But you don't have the attention span for me."

My fingers brushed his as I took the bottle back. "Never have I lost interest in you, my friend. But perhaps at times our self-interests clash with one another."

He snorted in either amusement or agreement. And then I was startled to feel his hand over mine, lightly brushing Minnie's curl with his thumb as I held it loosely. "I'm glad you came back," he whispered roughly.

"Remarkably selfish or selfless. One or the other," I replied.

"No, just remarkable." His hand grabbed my jaw. "Like you."

I shook my head for a moment in disbelief, but I sure as fuck wasn't going to talk myself out of what I was about to do. I tossed the box and the ribbon of curls into the ash and collided my lips with Ames's. His kiss was all bite and violent passion. None of the sweet shit he reserved for Blythe. No restraint of his power or want was afforded me… and I fucking loved it.

We were a tangle of grunts and desire as our bodies pressed

into each other. He pulled off my shirt as I yanked off his belt. The various beams of marred wood pricked into us, and I was fairly certain my leg was bleeding, but I didn't care. Pain was nice, though pleasure was better, especially amongst grief.

His fingers cut into my hips as he pushed my jeans down. I pulled away from his kiss and grabbed his jaw, mirroring his signature move. Tilting my head, I flashed my fangs. "I'm going to drink you, demon. But first, you're going to drink me."

His answering smile was devilish in acceptance of my challenge as he dropped to his knees, pumping my cock with a callused hold before sliding those gorgeous lips over my head. He swirled his tongue over my precum, and I tightened my grip in his hair. "Oh, let the demon out to play. You know I've missed it."

His laugh was brash, but then I felt it. The long, forked tongue of the archdemon. It glided down my shaft before coiling around my cock like a snake and squeezing. "Fuck," I groaned, tilting my head back. "Fuck, Ghost." The feel of his long tongue milking me, tasting me, squeezing, made me come embarrassingly fast, and I thrust my hips at his face, shoving my cock down his throat. The fucker wouldn't gag, though, would he? He only swallowed greedily, pulling off and wiping his mouth with the back of his hand. "Blythe and Wolf not servicing you well enough, I take it? Pretty quick there, my friend."

"Oh, my turn," I growled with a smile. "Let's see how well you take a vampire bite. See how long you last."

He raised an eyebrow in challenge, and I pushed him. "Lay back, you smug motherfucker."

Ames mock bowed. "Yes, your highness."

"Fuck off," I chuckled, feeling my mood lift significantly. "I'll make you call me your king, though. Count on that, archdemon."

He put his arms behind his head, looking like gold amongst a pile of garbage. Always too fine for his surroundings. Too lethal, too much of everything, really. I kneeled between his knees and bared my fangs. "You'll just have to wonder." I dipped and took him between my lips with a harsh suck. He hissed as I pulled off with a pop. "When will I strike?"

He growled low in his throat, pulling my hair. "I'm trembling in anticipation. But you talk too much. Get to work."

An order I would obey with eagerness. I gripped his thighs as I lowered my mouth around him, lapping against every black bead of his salty offering. Demons tasted like evil incarnate. It was a specific tang, a bite like scorpion venom. It was addictive. I'd been drunk off Ghost for centuries. I'd loved him, wanted him, and allowed our ebb and flow of desire and cooling, arguing and making up. This was our way. It was dysfunctional in all its loving acceptance of each other. And every time he came back to me like this, I felt a flurry of excitement, like I wanted to hold on to him like this forever. Could I suck him off enough that he'd be with me as constant as my werewolf or my reaper? Probably not, but I'd sure as hell try. And I knew that, regardless, if he drifted again, I'd be here waiting for him to come back. Ghost always came back to me.

Moving my touch as his cock hit the back of my throat, I cupped his balls, rippling my fingers as I felt them tighten near his climax. Bastard *was* lasting longer than me, but fuck it, this was fun.

Slowing my pace, I allowed my fangs to graze his length. Each down pump pressed them in a little harder. His grip tightened in my hair just as I cut the skin, his blood hitting my senses like an avalanche of the blackest parts of hell.

"Fuck, Onyx," he gritted out, shoving his hips forward, desperate for the release I held in my mouth.

"That's it," I chimed, sucking at the dripping cuts of blood on his cock. "Call me your king, and I'll consider letting you come down my throat."

He growled, and I smiled in accomplishment at the words that his pouty lips. "Fuck me, my king."

I struck then, with the speed of a vampire and the precision of a hawk. My fangs buried into his thick cock, and an explosion of cum shot into my mouth. It mixed with blood and heat and all the sorrow of the underworld that lurked inside the evil that was my lover. Sucking it all from him like poison, I drank his black seed, his thick blood, letting the waves of ecstasy burn me like the whiskey did.

Ames was my whiskey. There was no moderation with him. I was an alcoholic for the archdemon, needing all or nothing. Left wanting between relapses, knowing I could never quit him, knowing I'd never get enough. He called me his king, and I was, but he was mine, too. And maybe he was right, and this pile of broken shit could be our kingdom.

Our kingdom we built and ruled together.

CHAPTER 20

Wolf

PLAY THE GAME

Everyone was served. The light was too low to build or mend tonight, and I was on my way to patrol when I found myself standing in a square made of sticks. A small voice asked, "Wanna play foursquare?"

I didn't have the time, but then the pup added, "We're down a player since Lycus disappeared."

"He didn't disappear. He was taken by the monsters, dummy," the little girl with freckles corrected.

Fuck.

"Let's play," I said, clapping my hands.

So I did. And we played several rounds as Fenrir went awash in darkness. Soon, their parents called for them, giving me a wave as the pups grabbed their ball and sprinted toward their homes. We'd lost a pup, one of their friends. Lycus. I didn't realize my claws were pricking the skin of my clenched palm until blood trickled down my knuckles.

Where had the elders gone, and how did the lunas not return from their search for them? No traces of bodies, no scent trail left behind. It was as if they'd vanished, leaving the riff raff of chaos and darkness to descend upon our little sanctuary. I thought of the limp bodies of the foxes and imagined the wolf pups. It was an effort to keep the alpha locked inside.

The full moon was approaching, and I was losing my grip on my sensible nature. What havoc would I bestow when he took the reins? His fury rolled through me like a wave on the ocean, and it was only a matter of days before a tsunami crashed into us all.

I took some time to run through some training with the adolescents. The luna teens were swifter than the sols, but I was sure the boys would catch up with time. They were eager to get involved, and though they were younger than we typically allowed for this sort of pack work, I didn't have another option without the full strength of our lunas and elders to guide and protect us. I ran the perimeter, finding no traces of creature filth, and scented Onyx at the entrance, with Blythe breathing deeply on his chest, the same as they'd been every night this week.

My loves.

The white luna intercepted me. "I like your mate," she declared. "She suits you, and she's wise beyond her years."

"Thank you. And thank you for taking her under your watch today. I think it's been good for her spirit to be in the woods and be around lunas for a while."

"Of course. Have you considered the fact that she has no universal scent? Being invisible to the darkness, it's almost as if she is the darkness herself."

"It's something we know about her, yes." Where was she going with this? I tuned in to Blythe, hearing her slow heart and deep breathing. Asleep on Onyx and out of earshot.

Nephele scanned Fenrir and crossed her arms. A true leader, always keeping score, always alert. She'd grown on me during our time here.

"The elders and lunas similarly went beyond our senses. Without a trace, they vanished into the wilderness. No blood, no marks in the dirt showing struggle. I tracked their paw prints myself—the prints simply stopped. So did the scent."

"How does that involve my mate?"

"If she is the dark, perhaps she can find them within it. And her masking would make her hard to seek out."

"She's being hunted, threatened, on a near constant basis."

"Yet they cannot get to her. They don't see or smell her. They're guessing. Shooting arrows into the night, hoping to pin her. And this latest threat, the foxes? I can't help but mull over the irony that Blythe is a fox in a hole, and these measures are meant to smoke her out."

I huffed, feeling agitation tense my shoulders. "You're suggesting we allow them to draw her out? And what, waltz her over the mountain to follow a dead trail?"

"Not we, per se, but perhaps if she went alone—"

"Enough." I stopped her. "No more talk of that."

"But—"

"Send your own mate into the cursed woods alone and then talk to me about doing the same, Nephele. The answer is no."

I stomped over to where Onyx shot me an equally annoyed glance.

"Any news?"

"Nothing of consequence," he mumbled, petting Blythe's hair as she slept. "She's safe. That's all that matters. And that luna's idea is ludicrous. Could you imagine?"

Before I could respond, we both heard and felt him stalking through the brush. No attempts at silence or stealth. Ghost's smell was nearly indiscernible. Demons didn't smell like much, especially the highest-ranking ones like Ghost. Ghouls, on the other hand, smelled like absolute shit. No, Ghost smelled like hollow ground and holy water. There was much buried within the cemetery of his soul, and all of it was righteous and steadfast for his family, his home, and now his Claimed, Blythe. Our friend and leader emerged like an apparition from the shadows, flexing his hands and smelling strongly of blood that did not belong to him.

He'd done this each night this week, this same scene transpired. Usually he'd sulk off to shower, but this night he stopped.

"Have a nice day, honey?" Onyx goaded, still playing with Blythe's hair. But what was more disconcerting than the smell or the agitation that hadn't waned was what he told us.

"They're multiplying with each kill."

CHAPTER 21

Blythe

THE CHASE

Days later, I warmed my hands at Onyx's black blaze as the guys argued about how I'd be trained. My vampire gave up, exasperated, and kissed at my neck instead. I giggled at the sensation of his teeth as they tickled my sensitive spot. "You're insatiable," I teased, but he knew as well as I did that so was I.

"Oh, but your bite marks are my favorite accessories," he whined, pulling me flush to his chest.

"Why haven't you told the guys about your house?" I asked randomly, remembering one of our conversations during the week's night watch. My heart broke for him. His home was destroyed, along with all of his various collections of vintage items. I still had the T-shirt he'd given me on Halloween, and I was sad to know that the stash where they came from was now a pile of ash.

He shrugged. "I have my secrets. Even from them. And I know you have yours, too, don't you?"

"What is that supposed to mean?" My heart almost stopped. Could he have known about my biggest, meanest secret with an affinity for red and blackberries?

"I always know when you're lying." He winked. "You could stand to get better at it. Remember, the best lies aren't lies at all. Just twirling words about."

Ames called our attention, and luckily, I was able to break away from Onyx. Who knew which of my emotions he was picking up on as I narrowly avoided the topic of deception. Which reminded me, and worried me. Where had my mysterious antagonist gone?

"Wolfgang, grab her from behind," Ames instructed with no warning or preamble.

"Hey!" I protested, but it was too late. The werewolf had already lifted me off my feet and was holding my arms at my sides. "Okay, not fair. He's huge, and I had no warning."

"Won't be small, friendly monsters shouting warnings at you, little one," Wolf growled low in my ear, pricking the hair on the back of my neck with heat from his breath.

Onyx complained, "Keep turning her on, and none of us will make it out of here tonight."

"We need to see what she's capable of." Ames rubbed his temples, his black hair furling around his eyebrows. "Try to hurt him, little ghost."

Wolf gave me a squeeze, kicking the breath from my lungs. "Come on, luna, what're you going to do?" he chided gently.

I squirmed and kicked, but it was no use. I was dead meat, and this was pointless. "I can't win against you guys. You're, like, each deadly freaking comic book villains."

"At least she's acknowledging we're the bad guys, not the dopey heroes," Onyx sniped. "But this won't work. I'm sensing no fear from her. Only arousal. Which, trust me, I'm a huge fan of. But we know we won't hurt her, and she knows that, too. Unless she can get scared and we can get a little dangerous, we'll never be able to test out what she can do when pushed. Where her abilities will take her."

Wolf let me go, thumping me to my feet, and I inhaled, looking over the guys, remembering how the luna wolves had shown me to assess prey. The Halloween Boys were each deadly but good-hearted. At least mostly. Each had his own tastes and preferences, each was crazy about me, and each of them… I took a step back, and despite their being focused on their bickering, each set of eyes shot up at the small but meaningful movement.

"Oh, I see." I smiled, taking two more steps back. "I think I know how to get you guys not to hold back… and I think I know how to get me afraid."

They each inched forward, almost like they couldn't even control it. Ghost, Dragon, and Wolf were each entirely different, yet they had a common predatory instinct that drove them to seek me out, to hunt… to chase.

"You sure you want to do this, luna?" Wolfgang growled. "You might get more than you bargained for."

"I'm counting on it," I replied, kicking off into a sprint. "Just give me a head start, please!" I requested, dodging behind a tree and taking a hard left. There was one spot I wanted to go, and it wasn't terribly far, but I wasn't sure I could make it before someone caught me.

But something about running and the way I heard a flash of wind and the scraping of pebbles accomplished what I'd thought it would. Despite knowing they wouldn't harm me, I was afraid. Maybe fleeing made me feel like prey, and maybe it solidified their hunter instincts. As I weaved through trees, I remembered running from Ghost in the very place I was headed. My world had been shocked open upon a gravestone in October. A world of horrors and evils had emerged, and dammit it if I didn't love every second of it. And the devil was right about something. I was getting stronger. I could feel it in my bones. I could feel it in the quicker way I was running, like a weight had been lifted, like an arrow released from a bow. My abilities were dark and thrumming at the surface. I just needed the bravery to reach out and take them as mine. Claim them, claim myself as my archdemon had claimed me.

There was no deciphering between excitement and fear as I slipped over gravel stones and neared my foggy destination.

A beautiful laugh echoed around me. "My belladonna, you think you could ever be faster than me? You think I'd let my source of blood ever get away?"

My breath burned in my throat and down to my center. He was just watching me, waiting to attack. As I neared hell's gates, the creaky cemetery bars opened, allowing me inside. But just as I thought I'd have a moment to find a place to hide, something snaked around my ankles and yanked me backward. A scream fled my throat as I fell into the soft dirt. Blue smokey ropes coiled around my ankles flipped me over.

I kicked and struggled as a dark, foreboding figure appeared, looming over me. "Oh, little ghost, how foolish to run from me... from us..."

I pushed up on my palms, but the hold on my ankles only grew tighter as my archdemon, in all his shifted glory, pushed apart my knees. My heavy breathing wasn't from the run when he unfurled his long, forked tongue and softly tickled my inner thighs. I squirmed, not ready to lose in this game so quickly, when I spotted Onyx leaning against a tree, arms crossed and watching with a glowing green stare. My dark prince, my vampire king.

"Help me," I pleaded.

Ghost's tongue slapped against my pussy, making me yelp in surprise and pleasure, as Onyx sauntered over, not even out of breath from the chase.

Walking past Ghost, he stood over me, stepping over my chest. "I'll help keep you occupied while your demon makes you come. How about that?"

Before I could respond, my panties were ripped from under my dress, and I was filled in every way, all at once. As Ghost pressed a long, demon-shifted finger into my ass, I cried out, taking in Onyx's cock. The moan that vibrated against him intensified at the feeling of my demon's thick, wet tongue sliding into my already wet and wanting entrance. It wiggled and twirled and moved in a hypnotically sexy way, while the sensation of having every hole full of two men sent me into a pulsing and intense orgasm.

Onyx hit the back of my throat in time with Ghost, who filled me past the point of pleasure and pain with only his expert tongue. But just as Onyx was nearing his release, I closed my eyes and moved my ankles, realizing I was free. Had Ghost let me go, or had I undone my hellish ties somehow? It didn't matter, because I let him out of my mouth and slipped out of both of their grips. Giggling like a maniac at their groans of annoyance and protest, I took off running again, zigzagging between gravestones, hoping no spirits were floating by to witness the scene that was unfolding. Jumping behind a crypt to catch my breath, a low sound pulled my attention. Looking around, I didn't see anything, so I stepped out of my hiding spot—when suddenly something pummeled into my back, throwing me into the plush, wet grass behind the tomb.

A rough hand grabbed on to the back of my neck, not allowing me to sit up or even turn around. His other hand pulled me by the hips, ass in the air, and the growl turned deadlier, hungrier. "This ass," he gritted out, stinging it with pain as he slapped it. My dress had long been torn and fell down my lower back. The air hit all my wet and recently tasted parts, shivering me with cold sensitivity. "How can you let me chase you like that and not expect me to fuck you harder than you've ever been fucked?" Wolf rumbled lowly, and my core pulsed with need. "I'm throbbing for you," he hissed, pulling out his cock and sliding the length down the middle of my ass. "Feel it?"

"Please," I begged. "I want you so bad." I tried to turn my head, but his grip stayed firm, pushing my cheek into the grass. "You're so strong," I whimpered, knowing I stood a better chance of escaping from Ghost's chains of smoke or Onyx's fangs than I did from Wolf's immeasurable force. He vibrated a wild sound low in his throat as the wetness from the tip of his cock slid down my center and aligned with my wanting pussy. Another plea died in my tone and morphed into a cry as he impaled me with one swift movement. He'd always eased in before, let me be in control of taking him at my pace, but not this time. There was no warming up, no chance for my body to adjust to his girth. He impaled me with speed and fury, knocking the air from my lungs and pushing me into the ground. Voices sounded behind me in reverent and breathy tones.

"Fuck, look at her," Onyx admired. "She takes you so good, Wolfgang."

"Scream like that again," Ghost purred. "Let's hear how you sound as you come on werewolf cock."

I whined against a mouthful of bitter grass, feeling the dirt tangle my hair, knowing I must have looked awful. But the guys weren't deterred in the slightest. My hips bucked and jerked against him, pulling out with wet sounds that echoed through the graveyard. He forced himself back in, pushing embarrassing sounds from my throat.

His hand tightened on the back of my neck as he gritted out, "I think breeding you from behind, painting your lily pale skin with soil and cum, is my new favorite."

That rough and wild voice combined with the curve and hit of his cock undid me, and I broke around his explosion of wetness that filled my core. My hips bounced back as both of his grips tightened through the howl that fled him while he emptied into me, pushing in to the hilt. The now familiar stretch fought against the tightening flutters of my walls, knotting against my body's protests. I sucked in a deep breath, not knowing if my face was wet from sweat, the grass, or tears.

"Watch his knot stretch her, keeping all of his cum inside," Onyx awed behind me. "Aren't they magnificent together?"

"Too big," I complained. "I can't." I was out of breath and aching, and the burn was almost unbearable as it paired with my pleasure, pushing me toward yet another pulsating ripple of ecstasy.

"You can take the pain and stretch of him, little ghost. Haven't I taught you that?"

"Maybe she needs reminding," Wolfgang growled, rotating his hips so his knot shoved and pulled against my pussy lips.

I groaned in the fire of pain and desire.

When Wolf's knot eased out of me, creating a slippery mess, I moved to get up, but a large hand landed over my back. "My turn, little ghost," my demon growled. "And I'm not going to be gentle, either."

"I'll clean them up, lick them off you, and suck your blood straight from your cunt after, my belladonna," Onyx promised, kneeling by my head and moving the hair from my face as Ghost mounted behind me. I winced as he lined himself up, realizing that he was indeed much bigger than Wolf, even with the knot. This was going to hurt. This was going to feel amazing.

I wouldn't have expected any less.

I didn't want any less.

My monsters were mine, and they'd forever give me every bit of pain and torment I so desperately desired from them.

CHAPTER 22

Ghost

MY SKULL PAINT IS BETTER

> Beware of false prophets, which come to you in sheep's clothing, but inwardly they are ravening wolves.
>
> *Matthew 7:15*

The Bible had much to say about wolves. I'd studied the text for much of my existence and absorbed countless sermons. Something about the holy word stayed the same throughout hundreds of years, and there was comfort in that fact. Even if I was on the wrong side of the heavenly gates. But I disagreed with the stories about wolves. They weren't conniving, bloodthirsty beasts. What I'd seen of Wolfgang and his pack of Fenrir was a deep loyalty and respect for the world around them that transcended any trend or modern notion that had come and gone in my time being stuck as an immortal.

And somehow, while I slowly devolved into more of a wretched demon, Wolfgang grew finer, stronger, better. I supposed I should envy him, but it was difficult to do much more than stand in wonder of him and our profound differences. Though the current discord within Fenrir, the missing elders, their young taken under their noses, did remind me of one Bible story. The one that talked about wolves in sheeps' clothing deceiving the flock. It floated in my mind as my large and agile friend worried at the tint of the rounding moon.

"I'm losing my grip. I thought I could never hurt a woman, but I did. I hurt her, and the chase… fuck, it could have gone so much worse. And I'm looking down the barrel at turning again. Doing it again. And I won't be able to stop myself as the alpha."

Onyx hummed on a harmonica he'd found stashed away some-place as he reclined near the fire in Wolf's backyard. "Have you considered that she likes pain? Didn't my exceptionally pleasur-able bites, which you have also partaken in, prove that?"

Wolf snorted, more easily agitated the closer we got to the full moon. I'd admit, his alpha form intrigued me. I wondered how strong he'd get. I wondered if I could take him in a fight. If it came down to protecting Blythe, I'd be forced to.

"You probably pressured her into that. If blood wasn't your proclivity, would she have ever initiated such a thing herself?" he snapped.

"Agreed," I said.

Onyx polished the instrument. "I'm offended. If I sensed any hint of resistance, I'd stop in an instant. I thrive off consent."

"That's my problem. How do I get consent for what I don't know if I'll do or not?" Wolf slumped next to me on a log.

"Talk to her," Onyx encouraged, placing a hand on his friend's knee.

I hummed. "Or…"

The werewolf turned his attention to me. "Or what?"

Onyx raised an eyebrow, suddenly focused on the conversation at hand.

"Lock yourself up. Keep away from her on the full moon. If you're truly not sure how far you'll go, what you might do, then you are indeed a danger to our Claimed and to yourself."

The vampire huffed. "Oh, come on. Listen to you two. We're monsters. This shit is what she signed up for."

Ignoring him, Wolf asked, "Would you help me? Take me someplace without telling me where, chain me with hell smoke?"

Onyx dropped his jaw in shock. "No, absolutely not."

"I'll make it happen," I replied to my large, hairy friend.

Whining, the hybrid complained. "So you guys are just ignoring me now? Don't I get a vote?"

But it was too late. Wolfgang and I were shaking hands.

"Glad we worked that out," he rumbled. And that was our plan. A plan we wouldn't share with our mate.

When Blythe returned from the lunas the next morning, she'd dressed and eaten, and I employed a plan of my own. We'd all quickly taken to filling in the gaps of need in Fenrir. Onyx helped with cooking and tending the livestock. I'd been assisting Wolf in mending roofs and construction. And Blythe had been helping the lunas on their security rounds. We'd been busy, and though I loved my polyamorous group, I still desired private time with my Claimed. And she needed a break, perhaps a dangerous, fear-filled break. Wouldn't that be delightful?

I cornered her on Wolf's front porch as she was lacing up her brown hiking boots. "I'm taking you out, little ghost."

She raised a skeptical eyebrow. "Out where?"

"Come jump on my bike, and I'll tell you about it." I smirked, passing her her black and white skull helmet.

"Are you asking me on a date, Dr. Cove?"

I put my arm around her, loving the way Fenrir's woods made her hair smell like pine. Also loving the way Dr. Cove sounded on her sweet little lips. Before I could speak, the vampire interrupted, the werewolf on his heels.

"That's so sweet. Where are we going?" Onyx chimed in.

"*Blythe and I* are going to the circus. I hear there's a thrilling new act, and I'm dying to meet the ringmaster."

Blythe's eyes went wide as she looked up at me. "Seriously? You want to take me with you to talk to Zyre?"

Wolf grumbled. "Sounds dangerous. Shouldn't we all go?"

"You can't leave Fenrir right now, and I want to test a theory I'm working on with this chaos magician. It'll work best if we split up. And furthermore, I don't need to explain myself for wanting to take my girl out, do I?"

Blythe giggled, giving both Wolf and Onyx a quick kiss before tugging on her helmet. "We won't be long," she assured their dramatically pouty faces.

"Don't wait up," I winked, marching my little ghost to my motorcycle, pleased that my attempt at some alone time with her had worked flawlessly. It would be risky, waltzing into the chaos magician's territory with her, but their strength wasn't even close to mine. And we needed intel and a meeting with their head clown. Perhaps I could even talk some sense into the assholes. Stranger things had happened. If the circus left town and took what I suspected were their monsters with them, Wolfgang and I could return to normalcy.

But also… a night out with her, just us, sounded quite nice. She asked to stop and change, which was my thought as well, so we revisited my attic in Lamb's Blood Church. It looked exactly the same, and Father Joseph didn't bat an eye at my time away. The stained glass calmed me, and though Fenrir was charming, this was gloomy and cold. The way I liked it.

Blythe sighed in contentment. "All my makeup is still here. My heels, my clothes. All perfect." She hugged a black dress. "I'm excited to go on our first date."

I chuckled, buttoning my black shirt. "It's not our first date."

"First official one," she argued. "So, I'm wearing black gloss tonight and pumps."

"That sounds lovely, whatever that means."

"What is hell like? You've been, right?"

Her inquiry surprised and perplexed me. I raised an eyebrow,

"It depends on what level of hell. Some are less terrifying than others."

"And Devil, Judas, he lives there, rules it, I assume?"

"Indeed. Why?"

She dabbed her lips with something shiny and assessed herself in the mirror. "No reason."

When she was dressed, we argued about dinner. Eventually, I let her win. She chose fast food tacos, noting her reasoning was that she was tired of fancy vampire food and smoked meats, which was understandable. Ash Grove was lacking in the fine dining arena anyway. We arrived at the big top at dusk, and the place was a flurry of activity. Their tent was planted firmly in cinderblocks. Poles were dug into the earth, and trailers along the perimeter housed performers. The circus had been in my town for way too fucking long. And I was going to find out what they were after and how and why that involved my Claimed.

Blythe looked stunning in her short skin-tight black dress. Every curve of her voluptuous form was on full display. She'd twisted her hair up in a loose and tempting way, and the black lipstick begged for my cock.

"Your lip color reminds me that I want to paint your mouth that color later," I whispered in her ear as we entered the main tent.

That lovely blush of hers spread across her cheeks while honey invaded my mouth. She laced her arm in mine. "Only if you let me handle Zyre."

"What?" I questioned. "Far too dangerous."

"I have an idea, and I want to try something. Please, just trust me?"

My urge would always be to shield her, to make her my goddess on a throne who never needed to lift a finger. But to be my goddess truly, I'd have to let her do her bidding and make her commands and requests, and I'd find a way in my wretched heart to adhere to them.

So despite the overwhelming urge to argue and the rising rage I felt when I sensed the phantoms enter the ring, I only squeezed her tiny hand and nodded. "I trust you, little ghost. But I will obliterate anyone in your path if I sense even the faintest hint of trouble."

"I'd expect nothing less of my archdemon." She sighed sweetly, resting her head on my shoulder after we found our seats. "Is Vincent here?" she asked as the lights lowered.

"No, he's in Belladonia, either vying for the crown or for Onyx's mother. It would appear the ringmaster is now this Zyre asshole."

She tilted her chin. "That's him over there, in the white makeup."

I spotted him. He looked like no one special, and he sure as fuck couldn't paint on a proper mask. "My skull paint is better."

"It definitely is." She patted my hand, soothing my fragile ego. "His is more deranged mime. Yours is a work of Halloween art."

I smiled despite myself, pride stroked, and we watched the show. Nothing untoward happened. It seemed innocent enough, though I knew that couldn't be the case. Something sinister had to be lurking behind their operations. Why Ash Grove? Why threaten the wolves and pine after Fenrir? What part did they play in the ghouls' and diphyllas' arrival and lack of survival instincts? And most importantly, why was Blythe's name on the rotten breath of every monster in the forest? The ringmaster blew sparkles, and a horse appeared, bringing the crowd to a standing ovation.

Blythe was still short, despite wearing heels, so she pulled me down by my collar, and her lips met mine. Her tongue flicked into my mouth, and I could have fucked her right there in front of everyone. All I wanted to do was bend her over and pull that tight little dress over her ass and have her.

But she pulled away, breathing over the cheering crowd. "You always taste like honey." She pulled out of my grasp, and I had to fight my every instinct not to grab her and force her to stay. "Trust me," she said over her shoulder. "I love you."

And I loved her, too. Love was difficult for an archdemon. It wasn't something I had much experience with. But the church I haunted taught that love was patient, love was kind, and that love always trusted. Trust was love. And Blythe had my love, so she'd earned my trust. So I waited and watched her leave, clipping down the stairs as Zyre looked on at her like a hungry lion. Because I loved her so, I let her go.

CHAPTER 23

Blythe

JOKER

Freeing yourself was one thing, claiming ownership of that freed self was another.
Toni Morrison

Maybe spending my time with some of the most villainous guys in the world had emboldened me. Maybe every time I had run from a creature, monster, or situation was starting to fuel my steps forward. But all I could think about when I walked down the stairs in the muggy air of the tent was how, in October, I was running from a man in my past, and now, eight months later, I was walking toward another man that was chasing me and those I loved.

The phantom brandished his gaze over me and tipped his top hat. His face was white with heavy paint except for the black diamonds that washed over his eyes. As I opened my mouth to speak, he lifted a finger to silence me.

"Pick a card," he said, holding out a worn deck.

The crowd cheered, and the lights rose. The show was over for them, but it was only beginning for me. The smell of smoke wafted off the chaos magician, burning my nose. Patrons shuffled by as I pulled a card and Zyre put a hand theatrically over his eyes. "Don't show me. Let me guess."

"A man who likes games. How refreshing."

He puffed out a breath, shaking his head. "Two of spades?"

"Why are you here, and what do you want with Fenrir?"

He lowered his arm. "What's the point in talking to you— what's your name again? You're, what, their whore of the moment?" The phantom swept a glance over my shoulder, where I could feel Ames's stare burning my back. "Is this some game of theirs, sending you? Let the men talk, sweetheart."

"I'd believe the act if you weren't after me, attacking Fenrir, setting up camp in Ash Grove, and sending ghouls to do your bidding. That's you, right?"

"Six of clubs?" He spun on his heel and whistled. "I'll tell you what. Be a good girl and come find me without one of your gang members with you, and we'll chat. In the meantime, how many kids are left in Fenrir? Two, three?"

Raven had told me over and over again to trust my instincts. In that moment, I decided to listen. I grabbed the chaos magician's wrist, such an innocent movement, but the surge of dark power that thrummed through me was anything but. Black fog swirled around us, and when it cleared, we were back in the gray room I'd gone to with him when we first met and were searching for Onyx' lost family. That seemed like ages ago now.

Zyre looked around and crossed his arms. "Sure, by all means, step into my office. It's cute how your fire-man turns flames to different colors. I've tried with mine. I much prefer red, you see, but they always end up silver or black."

The confidence in his tone made me question everything. Had I done this, or had he? Who was pulling the strings? I wasn't as sure as I was at the beginning of our confrontation. Or maybe without the security of Ghost in my corner, I was weaker.

He paced the room slowly, twirling occasionally. "I'm guessing this is precious time for you, and we're only moments away from the demon ripping through the fabrics of the realms to pry you free. So to answer your question, *what do I want?*" He chuckled. "Lots of things."

I widened my stance like the guys had taught me and watched his every move. "Start with Fenrir and Ash Grove."

"Bossy, bossy," he teased. "Ash Grove is lovely and so close to the werewolves' land. A place rich with resources that appeal to me and room for the circus to set up shop. It's perfect, really. And with the dogs' dwindling numbers, wouldn't they be happier scurrying off into the sunset?"

"Where are the missing wolves?"

"Ah, that I don't know. Next question." He snapped his fingers rapidly. "Come on, make it fun. Make use of our time together. The only unforgivable sin is being boring, and you're losing my attention."

God, I really hated this guy.

"Why are the ghouls hunting me? What do you want with me?"

He sighed. "Those aren't good at all, but fine, I'll entertain it. The ghouls are stupid, easily manipulated. Little harbingers of chaos, aren't they? And those horrid bat creatures. Oh, they'll find a way to snatch you up, no matter how many of them your demon boy kills. Their time of hoarding this place to themselves is simply over." He spun and stopped in front of me. His circling had me disoriented and dizzy, and I steeled my jaw as he tapped my cheek patronizingly. "And you? I don't want you, per se."

I raised an eyebrow. "You're delusional if you think they'll let you get away with anything you're planning."

He chuckled maniacally and extended his arms. "But I've already gotten away with it, and here you are, coming to me. Oh, *I want you*, they *want you*," he laughed heavily this time, mocking me by pretending to dry his eyes. "You truly believe the infamous Halloween Boys desire you? That they just happened upon a little human girl and fell head over heels in love? What's your villain name again? The Grim Reaper? Death itself? Something like that, right? No one quite knows how, but you are Death herself. And wouldn't you know, every immortal is under your spell. Because what's the one thing immortals want but can't have?" He twirled on his heel. "After centuries of living and boredom and the mundane sameness of life with no reprieve, they all want to call it quits. But they can't. After the thrill of riches and sex and youth fades, the unknown and unattainable darkness of afterlife calls to them. And that's what you are, am I right? It's not you, stupid girl." He poked out his lower lip. "Look at you, with your mousey little freckles hiding behind too much makeup and bland and boring hair. You don't believe they've seen better and fucked better women than you?"

My knees shook in my stupid, uncomfortable heels and my throat tightened. His diamond gaze noticed me falter and smirked again before continuing. "You see, I'm not under your spell, because I was once human. A human who, unlike your friends, *didn't* want death. Quite the opposite. I sought out a devil to learn dark magic. I was his apprentice for decades. I worked for my immortality. I trained my powers. They weren't handed to me like some. Death doesn't appeal to me, so I see you through the lens of truth, unlike the brutes you surround yourself with. You've convinced yourself that they love you when you're simply their plaything. How pathetic. Are you that desperate for affection that you'd accept crumbs from monsters?"

My breath caught in my chest. He'd spoken the fears I'd buried for months. When I'd asked the guys if me being Death was the only reason they liked me, they'd all denied it, and we'd dropped the topic. But... what if Zyre was right? Would they have wanted me without the allure of darkness that haunted me?

"Perhaps you're the delusional one, Blythe. Four of diamonds?" he asked, as I held back tears. "Oh dear, but I could use you. You could lend yourself to the ones who can do something with your power. In exchange, I'll leave your dogs and townies alone. Deal? Think about it."

A single tear of insecurity and doubt slid down my cheek. Zyre's stupid white-gloved finger smudged it away. "You thought we were playing with strength and big muscles like you and your boys were practicing? That's adorable. My games are those of wit, my dear. And I've held the cards the entire time. You may be Death, but I'm the ace of spades."

Bitter smoke-scented fog engulfed us again, only this time, it was tinted with glitter, and I found myself outside in the empty parking lot as day had long faded to night, clutching the black card in my hand. It may as well have jumped off the page and laughed in my face.

The ace of spades.

CHAPTER 24

Wolf

FURRY COMPANION

Vladimir Nabokov

"She won't tell me what's wrong," Ames said, stepping out of Blythe's tiny house. Yes, Blythe's house. The one I'd given her when she'd first come to Ash Grove in October. Why wasn't she in my house?

Onyx crossed his arms. "We could go kill Zyre now. See how long the ghouls chew on his head until he dies."

"Did the chaos magician touch her?" I asked, not ruling out my friend's idea.

Ames ran a hand through his hair. "She says no. Just that she wants some time alone. We were having a good time until she spoke with him. We're on the right track, though. The phantoms are behind everything here, it seems. They're watching us even closer than we realized previously."

"So are we murdering him now, or should we wait until it's dark to set the mood?" Onyx tapped his foot.

Ames sighed. "Blythe said for us not to touch him. I don't know why. This seems like something she wants to handle privately."

"Privately?" Onyx raised an eyebrow. "No being on this earth gets to make her feel this fucking sadness and inadequacy and live. It's potent; it's horrible; and I want to rip out his throat."

I'd always known Onyx to be an emotional fellow. It's partly why I fell in love with him. The depths of his feelings were compounded by his gift of sensing the emotions of those around him. But it often made him act on impulse. Anything to make the feelings stop, to silence them. And sometimes feelings needed to just be felt, like wounds we licked as wolves that only needed time to heal and no special treatment. It seemed to me that Blythe was a luna licking a wound of sorts.

Suddenly, her door swung open, and she marched down, parting us like a sea. We were all quiet, unsure, as she spun around. "I'm running some errands."

She looked so hot when she was angry. And in those high-waisted black yoga pants and crop top, I was panting with want for her. The full moon was growing closer, and I was growing hungrier by the day. She would be mine, all mine, tied and knotted to me again very soon. I just hoped Ghost's plan to lock me away at the height of my alpha craze would work and spare her the worst of it.

Onyx turned on the charm and put his arm around her shoulder. "I'll go with you. I love shopping."

Shrugging him off, she huffed. "No, alone."

Ames furrowed his brows. "Not happening."

"You're not in charge of me," she countered, and Onyx hid his chuckle. Either of us would have gotten punched in the gut if we'd spoken to Ames like that. But Blythe could quite literally get away with murder around him.

"I am," he said with finality. "And you know I am."

She opened her mouth to say something that no doubt would have made it worse when I chimed in to broker peace, as I tended to do. "I'll accompany you in my wolf form. No talking. Just think of me as a furry companion for the day."

My luna narrowed her gaze. "You're too big for the car."

"Take my truck." I tossed her the keys from the pocket of my jeans. "I'll ride in the back."

Before she could argue, I shifted into my wolf. Though I was much bigger than a Great Dane, I'd still accompany her through town. Wolves knew how to lie low, and either way, she knew I was coming with her, or I was coming in secret. At least this way, I didn't have to hide from her. She hadn't known that I'd been following her as a wolf since the moment she arrived in town. I'd always be her shadow, protecting her, keeping her safe, being a warm pile of fur and softness to catch her when she fell.

"Good boy," Onyx said, only mildly mocking, as he patted my head. I gave his hand a playful bite that meant *I love you, asshole* and followed our girl into my pickup truck. She cranked the old engine, and I made the bed shake by jumping in. The old speakers began blaring as she turned up Fleetwood Mac. *Oh, it was a Stevie Nicks day, was it? We were truly fucked.*

We made it into Ash Grove after stopping at a convenience store. Her plastic bag smelled like powder and sugar. Perhaps makeup and candy? I'd been making her meals and neglected her candy fix, dammit. I made a mental note to look up how to make homemade gummy bears. We then stopped in town, and I jumped out of the back and stood next to her. She was so small, so delicate.

She looked me up and down. "You could never pass for an ordinary dog, Wolf. You're massive and scary looking."

Sitting, I tilted my head to the side and let my tongue loll out of my mouth, eliciting that gorgeous grin I loved from her. Shaking her head, she bit her lip. "You're an idiot."

True, but she was smiling, and that's all that mattered. The sun warmed my black fur and glistened upon her skin. Her freckles got darker in the spring. I loved it. People stared as we made our way through Ash Grove. Blythe walked leisurely, like she wasn't in a big hurry. Did she just need to get out of Fenrir? My soul hurt at the thought. Were we too much for her? No, it had to be that chaos clown. God, what I wouldn't give to be the one who got to tear my teeth into his sides. Only the worst of the world could even fathom being hateful toward someone as precious as my sweet luna. Also, watching her drive my truck was… not helping my heat.

She stopped to chat with an elderly couple—I think I recognized them from the diner—then moved on to the magic store. She pulled the handle, and it didn't budge. Cupping her hands around her eyes, she looked through the window. "They're closed. Magia is never closed." She sighed. "I haven't seen Yesenia since being back."

I brushed past her, not missing the small movement of her fingers reaching out to graze my fur. Sniffing the door handle, I smelled the crone in all her patchouli and incense. Beyond that was a bunch of random smells, until finally, at the bottom, was the younger witch. Her lavender and amber scent was more pleasant. And then a scent trail snaked through the air like a ribbon. I nudged Blythe's elbow with my nose and couldn't help my tail wag when she scratched behind my ear.

Giggling, she asked, "What? Are you saying we should go that way?"

She'd understood the adolescent sols in their wolf forms, which was unheard of. I knew I could have spoken to her, but I promised to stay silent, so that I did. I nudged her again until we were back at the truck. I glanced toward her and then up toward the path toward the brew pump. She seemed to understand where I wanted her to go and agreed as I jumped in the back of my truck. The music blared through the fuzzy vintage speakers. *Queen this time. Maybe I was cheering her up.* We landed in the gravel parking lot outside where Hallows Fest took place, and I guided her up the path, smelling everything as I went. The trees were happy to see her again. Odd, I thought, but I couldn't blame them. I was always happy to see Blythe, too. Giving her space, I trotted ahead, crunching through brush and knocking sharp sticks or thorns out of her path. She followed gently, stopping to pluck something and striding to catch up and show me. Stopping, I sniffed it as she held it out, knowing exactly what it was before she told me.

"Lamb's ear," she said. "Like you showed me on our trip to the waterfall."

God, she is adorable. Not able to help myself, I licked her knuckle, and she laughed, wiping it on her pants. It wasn't hard upholding my promise to not talk to her. No, we were communicating just fine, my luna and me. And maybe a day with me in this form was helping her tend to her wounds in some way. The thought made me proud to be a wolf. I hoped I could be proud to be an alpha someday, too, and not constantly afraid of what I'd do when that form returned on the full moon. Would she still love and trust me after Laverna? Pushing the thoughts away, we stopped outside of Hell's Gates. It vibrated and thrummed a sound only wolves could hear, basically saying hello, like many things in the forest did when we passed by. Kneeling by the gate was the woman Blythe had been searching for. We'd been fresh on her trail.

"Blythe?" Yesenia asked, standing. "It's been so long." She opened her arms and they embraced.

"I went to Magia, and Marcelene—"

"Our coven split in two not long after you left," Yesenia explained. "Our ideals were too different. The crones and the newer witches… I wish it wasn't this way. But we can talk about that later. You're back. Oh my gosh, girl, what's up?"

"It's been a crazy adventure. One that's not over yet. The woods, the ghouls, and Fenrir—"

"I know. I wish I could do more to help." The gates shuddered and sighed, swooning over Blythe as I'd seen them do before. Creepy stuff loved her. "I was offering the gates mint before I entered. Cemeteries need offerings from witches, you know."

A meow sounded before a feline hopped off a gravestone and strutted forward. I let out a small huff, warning the surly creature to be kind to my mate, and the familiar and the witch regarded me, then.

"Wolfgang, nice to see you again," Yesenia smiled.

Cat licked her paw. "Yesenia, please tell your visitors today is not a good day to view my graveyard. They'll need to make an appointment and come another time."

"Cat," Yesenia warned.

Blythe kneeled and offered her hand. "We've been gone so long. She has every right to be angry. I'm sorry, Cat. I don't know what happened, but I'm sorry we disappeared. You've done a great job holding it together."

The animal eyed her palm, then walked up and gently rubbed against her wrist. Blythe pet her softly, and my heart warmed. She was great with animals. She was kind and gentle with everything. Blythe was just *sweet*. And apologies and flattery went far with cats.

We walked through the cemetery. Everything looked and smelled normal. The damned were still suffering. A few ghosts floated by; some stopping to say hi to Blythe. She was as gracious as she was with mortals, entertaining their questions, asking about their days. I enjoyed watching her and following behind her while she caught up with her witch friend and Cat listened on, no doubt to relay it all in her gossip to other familiars later. I sat under a tree, giving them their privacy, unlike one very nosy feline, until my ears perked up at the sound of a name.

"Zyre is shrouded in dark magic, and evil entities cling to him. Chaotic demons, the mayhem of hell. Be careful around him, Blythe. My new coven, the Medicine Thicket, has had interactions with the phantoms that haven't been… pleasant."

I straightened at that, reminded that the magic man needed to die, and soon.

"Then why have you and the other witches let them stay and get so involved in Ash Grove? They have something to do with the monster invasion and the pups going missing, along with the elders."

"The Moon Halo Coven has let them set up camp in Ash Grove. It's one of the things we had disagreements over before the coven split. My new coven, we are powerful, but in different ways from my abuela."

Blythe let out a breath, and Yesenia took her hand. "I am so sorry that after what you endured in Belladonia, you came home to find Ash Grove like this. I tried… I just wasn't enough."

"Home? So you guys aren't kicking me out again?" Blythe asked in a half-joking tone.

"Of course not, and that was never me or anyone in the Medicine Thicket anyway. Ash Grove is your home. It's as much yours as the Halloween Boys. You're a part of it now, this place." She looked around. "There's nothing else like it."

Blythe hugged her again, and they said their goodbyes. When my luna had returned to my side again, the witch turned and spoke to me. "If it means anything to you, Wolfgang, when I search for the elders and the pups in my mind's eye, they aren't on the other side. It's like they're still here but… stuck somewhere. Maybe someone"—she flicked a not-so-subtle glance at Blythe—"could find them and bring them home." I stood and bowed my head. The Halloween Boys didn't care for the witches, but I liked this one. "Oh, and one more thing. Bathe the pups in holly and put ash wood in their cribs at night. It should help them to not get stolen."

Why did witches always leave with such ominous parting words? Goodbye would have sufficed. I snorted, shaking out my fur. Witches assumed everyone wanted or needed their particular magic, but as wolves, we did not and would not utilize their gifts. Witches worked with the earth, us wolven—we were the earth. Holly and ash wood… I rolled my eyes.

We stopped at a fast-food burger place on the way home, and Blythe climbed into the bed of the truck with me, unwrapping several meat patties and laying them out before my front paws. She leaned against my side as she ate her fries, and we sat in silence, watching the sun set and wash Ash Grove in orange. She softly glided her fingers through my fur and cuddled against me, and I let her, knowing that sometimes that's all anyone needed. To lie down next to someone who loved them. Blythe knew I loved her. She had to.

When we arrived back in Fenrir, the fires were going, and Onyx was cleaning up from the dinner he'd made for the pack. My heart swelled at the knowledge that he'd taken that on in my absence. He'd served me and the pack in that way. He'd always been there for us, without asking for anything in return. Ames was chopping wood, and he paused with the axe over his shoulder as Blythe approached. Saying nothing, she gave him a kiss on the cheek, and he stopped her as she tried to walk away, grabbing her chin and bringing her mouth to his. Their apology, I guessed. Smiling, she then walked past her house and up the porch to mine as I pranced behind, still unsure of whether she wanted to talk. Ghost was on security duty tonight, so Onyx and I would stay with her.

She gave Onyx's hand a soft squeeze and paused in my door-way. "See you guys for bed soon?"

Onyx nodded. "Of course, belladonna."

When she'd gone inside and I'd shifted back into my human form, the vampire asked, "She seems better. So you talked to her?"

Looking toward my house that was now a home because of her, and the smoke coming from the roof where she was making a fire, I smiled. "Yeah, we talked. She's going to be just fine."

CHAPTER 25

Blythe

SOME NERVE

After sleeping nestled between my vampire and my werewolf, I woke the next morning feeling a bit less dreary. Before the sun was fully up, I'd slipped away to the kitchen cabin. Raven had been spending more time at his tree-house with the other familiars lately. It was good for him. I assured him I was safe and that he was always free to explore and pop in and out as he pleased. It was my turn to help with breakfast, and I was actually looking forward to quiet cooking time. But when I opened the door, my contentment, my hope, and my steady heart-beat vanished.

"Good morning," Devil said in greeting, cradling a mixing bowl as he stirred. "I was thinking muffins sound nice today, don't you think?"

I looked over my shoulder before giving my arm a pinch. He raised a quizzical eyebrow, and I glared. "Trying to wake myself up from this nightmare."

A dark chuckle echoed off the tile. "Toss those berries in flour, would you?"

His shirt sleeves were rolled up his forearms in that distracting way as he stirred the batter. The Devil was making muffins.

"I never know what to expect with you," I said, doing as I was told and sprinkling flour over a dish of freshly washed blackberries.

"I wouldn't be a very good devil if I was predictable, would I?"

Maybe it was the early morning hour, the crisp taunt of spring, the phantom still in my head, or the hilarity of baking with the devil, but I fell into my own thoughts as I buttered muffin tins.

As he filled them with a ladle, his soulful eyes swept over me. "More morose than usual."

"More nosy than usual." His answering amused scoff sent an unexpected wave of rage through me, and I tossed a dirty pan into the sink. "Are you going to help, finally? Because you only seem to show up to antagonize. But you know, there are people who could use your help. The wolves are good, and they don't deserve to live in fear and hardship like this. Ash Grove has been through enough and now the forest is full of monsters—"

He stepped toward me, and my heart leapt into my throat. "So what are you going to do about it, Mortala? Or have you already forgotten those glimpses of who you are?"

I swallowed a lump of emotion. "Our bargain was you help me in exchange for me keeping these encounters a secret. When are you going to help?"

He reached a hand forward and twirled a loose strand of my hair lightly around his finger. Without even touching me, the heat from my anger crashed into the butterflies in my stomach, both collapsing in my core. Maybe it was part of what he was, the allure, the beauty, but he was infuriating, mysterious and, for some reason, so freaking hard to resist.

"Encounter." He tasted the word slowly. "I like that. And I am helping."

"How?" I asked, embarrassed by the way it came out as breathless.

The oven timer dinged, and the side of Devil's mouth curved. "I made breakfast."

"Well, help more," I sneered, but the bite was gone from my words.

As the tension between us thickened and the strand of hair he twirled may as well have been my aching clit, the door slammed open, and the sounds of footsteps pattered into the kitchen.

"Muffins!" a little girl chirped.

Two little boys laughed and shoved at each other, searching the countertops for food.

"And meat, of course." Judas smiled, plating the pastries and hefty piles of bacon for the kids.

"Judas, play four square with us later?" the little girl asked. "Wolf is no good."

"Judas is even bigger than Wolf. How do you think he'll be any better?"

"Okay, kickball then," she countered.

The devil chuckled, dusting the muffins in powdered sugar. "You're on. I'll meet you after dinner, but only if you get your chores done."

They whooped and cheered before leaving in the same flurry of sound and laughter that followed children.

My jaw dropped. "They know you?" The kids didn't seem afraid of him. In fact, they seemed… very familiar with him.

After washing his hands, he rolled down his shirt sleeves and walked past me toward the door, a very un-devil-like exit. Where were the plumes of smoke and numbers left behind, counting down to something I was sure I didn't want to think about? "What are you doing?"

Pausing in the doorway that next to him made the regular-sized building look miniature, he replied, "Helping more."

MY HEART BEAT FURIOUSLY as I piled the muffins and meats in baskets and made my rounds, delivering breakfast to every stella, luna and sol. The pups were already busy building a fort in the middle of Fenrir, laughing as if there weren't dangers lurking everywhere. I guessed that was a sign of a good community. If the kids weren't afraid, they felt safe. And the wolves indeed felt like a safe haven, even in the midst of the terrors around us. When I was finished and had eaten one of the muffins myself, cursing the world at how delicious it was—*of course the devil could bake*—I went to find the guys, but stopped a few yards outside Wolf's cabin.

"That was a long time ago," Wolf growled, sounding angrier than I'd ever heard him.

I couldn't hear anything but a low tone from the person he was talking to. Suddenly aware of how loud my steps sloshed through the damp morning grass, I inched forward.

"I did what I had to do," Wolf lamented. "Though I regret it now, and I sure as hell regret getting involved with you."

When I turned the corner, I met the intense gaze of my werewolf, who was pacing like he did when he was stressed. And then the source of his stress turned to face me.

"Nice to see you again, Blythe. Been a while," the devil rumbled, hints of dark mischief dancing in his steely stare.

"What's going on?" I asked, my chest tightening and mind whirling as I took in Wolfgang's state.

"My fellow Halloween Boys asked for help. I'm here to help bail them out of trouble, yet again," Judas replied deeply.

Wolfgang snorted, joining my side and wrapping a protective arm around me. "Careful the assistance you accept from the likes of hell," Wolf murmured to me. "It's always deeper trouble than you were in before."

My heart clenched at his words. What sort of arrangement did he have with Devil, and did it mirror my own? It was then that I began to wonder what sort of separate webs we were all caught in. Was Judas even on our side?

"How did you guys meet?" I asked, surprising them with such a basic question packed with meaning.

Devil stared at Wolf, his gaze harsher than he'd used with me, and fear pricked the hair on my arms. I'd known he was dangerous, but I'd rarely seen that danger in action or felt it like I did then. Wolf tightened his grip around me and straightened. My werewolf would never back down. Not even from the devil himself.

"We met a long time ago, on Halloween," Wolf rumbled.

"Trick-or-treat," a sarcastic voice cut in. "Showing up late is so typical now, my friend. We should get you a watch," Onyx purred, stepping in front of me.

Before the devil could respond, blue fog wafted along the green of Wolf's backyard, and Ames appeared, looking dark and terrifyingly handsome. My boys would protect me, and I would protect my boys. The knowledge was a balm against all my uncertainty.

"Nice of you to join us, Ghost," Devil rumbled, quickly establishing his rank as the leader of the group. "Seems you made quite the mess of things."

Ames let out a breath, and I could tell he was calming himself down as he joined us. "You going to tell us what happened during our blood ritual in Belladonia or stick with the cryptic, quiet guy persona? Because frankly, we're busy."

In a flash, Devil grabbed Ames by the collar of his shirt, and I gasped, finding myself blocked by Onyx and held firmer by Wolf. Their first instinct was me over their archdemon friend, and I wasn't sure how I felt about that.

"You. Summoned. Me," Devil bit out. "And I wasn't invited to your little blood orgy in Vladimir's wicked city, so the fault is your own. It is your poor leadership, Ghost. This is what you do with the gifts I bestow? The secrets I keep and what they've cost, what they're about to cost?"

The guys froze around me, and Onyx's palms heated where one rested against my hip. Ames pushed out of the devil's grip and breathed heavily. "Why don't you enlighten me, Judas? Our lapses in memory seem to suit you until you choose to weaponize them."

"How about we fight this out before we talk?" Onyx suggested, his voice the picture of sinister smoothness. Sometimes his dragon made way for a snake, it seemed. "We haven't had a kill club meeting since autumn."

"Kill club?" I whispered to Wolf.

He only shrugged as Devil looked at each of them before boring his gaze into me. "Yes, and she's participating as well."

The only answer was a low growl vibrating from Wolf's throat, but no one argued. Maybe they couldn't argue. And the thought that my boys were afraid of anyone or anything sent chills down my spine. And I wondered, who was this Devil I'd been consorting with in private these past few months? And what did he want with me?

HUGGING MY KNEES, I cringed as I watched the carnage of blood and sweat before me. They were beating each other senseless, and between the grunts and falls to the ground, they assured me that they loved it. Men were weird. But it did seem to be helping their bad moods.

Except for Devil, whom I was secretly grateful to have an opportunity to examine. Every now and then, his sultry, evil-looking gaze would catch mine and I'd look away, hoping it wasn't obvious that I was staring. I didn't think any man could be bigger than Wolf or stronger than Ghost or swifter than Dragon, but it seemed Devil was there as their teacher, as the one strongest of them all, and they were learning from him. It was then the leader title made more sense. Because in actual interactions, they didn't communicate much at all, and the little they did speak, it was like code that I didn't understand.

When the training subsided and Ames sat next to me, splashing me with sweat, I took his jaw in my hands. "You're bleeding."

"I know. Isn't it great?"

Wolfgang and Onyx were caught between a duel and a lover's match, and I was eager to continue watching them. It was hot. But then Judas blocked my view.

"Your turn," he thundered, extending a leather-gloved hand.

I widened my eyes and looked at Ames. "He's not serious."

My archdemon tensed his jaw. "It's one of the reasons I asked him to come. His power matches yours more closely, Blythe. You're both entities of sorts… He can teach you things we cannot."

The corner of Judas's mouth lifted ever so slightly as he replied. "That I can, little reaper."

I don't know why my stupid, curious heart fluttered at that statement, but it did. I took his hand, and he pulled me to stand like I weighed nothing. We walked to the center of Fenrir's field until the guys were several yards away.

The devil took a few steps back, looking down at me with those ancient eyes. "You're good at lying to them. At pretending you don't know me."

My heart gripped in my chest. Panicked, I looked to the guys, who'd surely caught the exchange. But Ames was only flicking glances between us and Wolf and Onyx's match.

"Don't worry. I made it so they can't hear."

"I *don't* know you. What do you want?" I questioned, crossing my arms.

"You need to learn to ask better questions. The stronger the immortal, the shorter the attention span."

I rolled my eyes. "What is it you can teach me that will help Ash Grove and Fenrir?"

"That's mildly better," he grumbled. "You're smarter than you let on." Before I could reply, the ground shook, and red, glowing vines shot up from the grass. Fear and panic grabbed me alongside their barbs as they twisted around my ankles. "Break free."

I didn't want to show my fear, didn't want to let him know he scared me. He could already see right through me as it was. The red ropes burned my skin in that same horrifying way as—

Suddenly, another twisted around my ribs and snaked up my throat, squeezing my breath. I closed my eyes, knowing where I'd met these chains before. Feeling the life drain from my body, feeling tired and dizzy. All I could think of was the baphomet's rectangular eyes, the potion it poured… the vessense it made me drink… and then I saw her. Me—the horns. And I remembered.

Opening my eyes again, I stood up straight and stepped forward. The red ropes fell away like sand behind me. I looked to Judas for a response, but his face was impassive as he flicked a finger. And darkness surrounded me. I reached my hand in front of me, and there was nothing. Only black. A fear of a different sort took hold, and I couldn't even celebrate my victory of besting the chains of hell's evil.

Devil's voice echoed all around me. "Not all fights are brawn, dear girl. Not all battles are that of power or even magic. More often than not, pure nerve and a calm mind will do more for you than your tricks."

"I know that," I challenged, annoyed to be looking for an exit. Of course this little test wouldn't be so simple.

Judas hummed. "You let the magic man get in your head. You've let me get in your head. Your mind is yours to guard above all else. The blood of wars is child's play in comparison to the destruction of allowing a contemptible phrase into your mind."

"How do I not? How do I keep them out?" I asked, sincerely hoping he'd give me a real answer.

"All words are spells, and all spells should be acknowledged like a visitor in your home. But not all visitors are asked to stay. Some you should usher out as quickly as they came. The doors are everywhere, if you only look for them."

"Like Belladonia?" I asked, more to myself than anything. I wasn't sure why I thought of the vampire city just then, but the visual helped. Then the devil took form, crossing his arms before me. He cocked his head to the side. Looking to his left, I knew what I'd find. Was it because I'd created it? I gestured toward the door, and he smirked before giving me a bow.

"Better," he said before exiting. And then I followed after him, opening the door into the brightness of the open field again.

Wolf, Onyx, and Ames were there then, staring on with bewildered and concerned expressions.

"Where were you?" Onyx asked, wiping blood from his brow.

"I still don't know. Ask him," I answered honestly, looking to my right. But no one was there. "Where's Judas?"

Ames shrugged, still surveying me, as if to make sure I was truly in one piece. "He comes and goes."

"We might see him tomorrow or in five years. We never know," Wolf added. "Are you okay?"

"I'm fine," I replied, feeling a rush of endorphins. I'd done it. I wasn't quite sure what I'd done, but it was materializing now. The ability to walk through magic meant to harm me. The dark room, the doors… it was coming together like an abstract painting in my mind. The devil could have shown me anything, taught me anything, but he chose those today. And I felt it was for a reason, even if I didn't understand it immediately. He'd said I was smarter than I'd let on. And I was thinking it was time to start letting on. It was time to start being brave.

CHAPTER 26

Wolf

STOLEN

A yowl of sorrow pierced through the misty night air of Fenrir. It was earth-shattering and soul-crushing as it came from my throat. But it was not me. Not the me I recognized. And then paws were ripping into the earth as they propelled me forward. My arms were longer, stronger, more flexible. The full moon was closer, and my grip on my self control was slipping. But it wasn't the smell of Blythe's sex that had me tearing down the door and charging into the night. It was the stench of swamp and dead bats that woke me. Close. They were here.

Not only were they inside Fenrir as I awoke to see my mates wrapped in each other's arms, naked and safe. The ghoul scratched at the door, the same as they did for vulnerable humans to scare them at night. It whispered to me, wretched and serpent-like with its hisses that strived so hard to sound human. *"Give us Blythe. Give her to us, or they die. Your young will perish this night, Wolfgang."*

They fed on the fear like all variants of demons did. It didn't scare me. It enraged me. It insulted me. It woke the alpha. And I wasn't stuffing him back inside my chest. He got to run free, and they were fucked now.

The scent ribbon shot in multiple directions, twenty or more? How was that possible? Nephele and the adolescent wolves raced past me, each following a different ribbon, the pack working the way it should, better than it had when I'd first arrived.

I grabbed hold of the thickest scent string, racing, following it into the woods. It was still warm, and it was a big fucking demon who'd left it. He was toying with me, and it was time he died between my fangs.

Something snapped as I tore through the forest, upright now. Damn, walking as a werewolf was fun. I was tall, and I'd appropriated all the best features of my human form and my wolf form combined. It was feeling less like a curse now. No, it was feeling like a weapon. I was a weapon, an exaggeration of a hunter, the god of the hunt. And this motherfucker was my prey.

It was still running, thinking it blended with the darkness, as I reached the continuation of its trail. Wolf me would have been subtle, waited for my pack. Human me would have grilled it for information before killing it. But alpha me was a new breed. He commanded my blood with nothing but instinct. No talk, no thinking, no hesitation. Lunging forward, I took the creature's neck between my maw and jerked, hearing the snap. But I didn't stop as its black blood dripped through my fur. I ripped its head from its shoulders and tossed it into a thorn bush. And then a bat creature jumped onto my back, sinking wretched, deformed vampire fangs into my shoulder.

It would have slowed me for a moment if I were a wolf. Like it smelled me as. Like it expected me to be. But I wasn't just a wolf shifter anymore, was I? I stood, and its fear rippled off its scent and almost made me laugh as I used my clawed hands to rip off its jaw as it shrieked in terror. Two more ghouls decided to die, drenching me in their foul blood as I tore them to shreds.

More. The alpha demanded. *More, more, more.*

Another howl shook through me as my alpha rampaged. Hunting every trail, cutting every thread with death. My gashes didn't slow me. They only fueled my rage and my killing.

The darkness turned deep orange as I ripped another throat of a screaming demon. Something grabbed my shoulders. I turned, throwing the huge demon off me as his icy blue eyes glowed.

"You're done," he growled.

Friend, this one was my friend.

I slammed my fist against the trunk of a tree. Ha, I had a fist now. "I'm done when I say I'm done."

Another voice coaxed as he leaned against an oak, kicking the head of a diphylla with his boot. "Blythe needs you, big guy. So does Fenrir. Shit went down. Let Wolfgang back out, and let's go home."

Another roar that wasn't my own shook the branches and sent the birds into flight as I stomped behind them. Before I passed the threshold, I heard it. The worst sound imaginable. Worse than demon shrills and bone snapping. This sound was one that made me curse my heightened auditory function. Onyx winced, and I lowered next to my friends, Wolfgang again. The woman's cry rippled through Fenrir, and I ran to find her in the middle of our community, on her knees, holding a small blanket.

"No," I breathed.

Onyx dropped to his knees as well, holding his head. The pain I felt from her cry was indescribable. I could only imagine feeling it head-on, taking it in. Ames took Onyx in his arms and Blythe appeared, doing the same, stroking his hair.

"My babies." She rocked back and forth, sobbing. "The pups. They're only pups," she wailed. And the wolves that encircled her howled, a long and forlorn sound of anguish… and promise. Blythe looked up to me, tears streaking her face as she stood and joined the lunas, taking the crying mother's hands.

My mate pressed her forehead against the grieving mother's, finding her gaze through her tears of loss. The crowd hushed with reverence as she whispered a vow. One that echoed in all of our bones as wolven. A promise that terrified me more than the ghouls' hisses and threats.

She spoke with authority, echoing like the olden force I knew she was. "I'm going to find them," she breathed, and the crowd hushed with a sense of reverence. "And I will make anyone who touched them pay."

Death was speaking.

"My alpha won't allow what you're proposing. He can't allow it. It's too much. Too dangerous," I boomed to my mate and the onlooking pack. I hated my tone. It was shaken, rattled, unhinged.

But Blythe didn't back down. "I'm not asking for permission. We're all a part of this pack, right? And I'm invisible to these monsters."

"That's right," Nephele agreed, standing next to her. "It's time we do something."

I clenched my fists. "We are not placing this burden on my mate. She's not a wolf shifter. She can't kill a ghoul. And we're sending her out like a lamb to slaughter?" I looked to Ames and Onyx, who sat quietly by the fire. Onyx hadn't spoken, and the look of life-draining sorrow on his face made me pale in sadness. The pups were gone. How could this have happened?

The red wolf, Carmine, spoke up. "I think they're tracking you guys. The Halloween Boys. They know she'll be with you, so they launch their attacks near your crew, hoping to land her. If she goes and you stay, they won't suspect it."

"Yesenia said she sensed that the elders and the pups were alive. I'm going to find them."

I growled again, wanting to shake her. "Over the mountain alone? Even if I said yes, the alpha in me would hunt you down, and I don't fucking know what he'll do if he thinks you're running, Blythe. The ghouls aren't the only monsters after you—I am."

Silence accompanied the pops of fire in the air. I looked to Ghost and Dragon for agreement. Surely, they'd back me up. But Onyx wouldn't look at anything but his shoes. Shocked, heartbroken in the pit of his empathic abilities.

Ames rubbed the vampire hybrid's back before glancing at me and then Blythe. "If she thinks she can do it, the best we can do is support her. Even if it kills us."

I couldn't believe what he was saying. Ghost was almost as possessive as my alpha, and he was okay with letting her wander into the woods on a quest that might not even lead to where we wanted? He'd grown. Love had changed him. Blythe had turned him into a pile of mush.

Nephele spoke again, addressing the pack. "The phantoms have brought this on. They've infested our land with monsters. They've hidden our elders and stolen our pups. They want Fenrir. They want Blythe. They know without our pack at full strength, and leaving the Halloween Boys without their reaper, that we are all weak. We must make a stand. We must put things back together. As wolves, our pack, our community is our lifeblood, and we have to set this right. On this night, one week before our spring celebration of Laverna, Blythe is the luna who will free us."

"Think about it, Wolf." Blythe took my hands in her tiny grip, small palms that couldn't kill a fly if they tried. "Nephele is right. They're trying to take out Fenrir one by one. They want this place. They want my power. And they don't expect anyone to let me go. But I'm invisible, and I'm powerful. I can fix this. I can find the lost pieces and put this all back together." She wrapped herself under my arms in a hug, and I wanted to keep her there forever. "I'm your luna. I can be your wolf, too."

"Little Red Riding Hood is more like it," I grumbled. "Or we could go kill the phantoms now," I suggested. "What are we waiting for?"

Nephele answered. "We tried that and lost many wolves. They work in sickening magical practices. And if they die, the knowledge of where the elders are dies with them should we need it. But with our pack at full capacity, we could quickly eradicate them and their presence in Ash Grove, along with the ghouls, wherever their hidden source of generation may be."

"I think it's a door," Blythe answered her. "If it's a door, I can find it and close it."

Onyx sucked in a breath and offered Blythe a weary smile. "If anyone can, it's you, belladonna. We can't be the ones holding her back, Wolfgang. We've seen what she can do. She's strong."

I swallowed my possessiveness, my alpha rage, my caveman want to tell her no. As if it were my call to make. As if she were my property. But Onyx was right. Blythe didn't belong to us. If anything, we belonged to her. And she'd decided what she was doing, and it was in service of my people, of our people.

And wasn't that how I was raised? The women led while the men served. This was that within my own pack. My little family of Halloween misfits. She was not only *my* luna. Blythe was *our* luna.

CHAPTER 27

Blythe

TALK SHIT, GET HIT

> If you have ever been called defiant, incorrigible, forward, cunning, insurgent, unruly, rebellious, you're on the right track…
> *Dr Clarissa Pinkola Estés*

The guys were somber as we all settled into Wolf's cabin for the night. There was no arguing with me. I'd decided the moment that luna's cries brought my love to his knees in anguish. I'd decided the moment her tears stained my face as I held her in her sorrow. If I was mauled by ghouls and diphylla, then so be it. It didn't change the fact that I was going in search of the lost children. And in the process, I hoped to find the elders and the source of the ghouls coming to Ash Grove. There were eyes, like the witches had said before I'd journeyed with Onyx. There were eyes all around me, watching me. So many eyes, they said. Well, they could watch me as I brought balance, because I was done running and hiding from them.

Wolf was mad at me. I could tell. I was defying him, as the alpha, by doing this. Any other wolf would have probably been eaten up for challenging him the way I did. But it was just another reason why it had to be me. Why it made sense that I would be the one to take this task on. Wolfgang began stuffing things into a bag for me. Jerky, fruit, water, socks.

The lunas and I had decided I'd leave in the morning, and fear mixed with hope so vigorous that Onyx caught my glance and flashed a soft smile. "You've got this, Belladonna."

Ames only sat quietly next to him. I knew the look on his face. Knew he was warring with himself. Over who he was, who he is, and who he wanted to be for me. I was just about to curl up on his lap when a knock rattled the door.

We all stopped, and Wolf inhaled. "Oh, fuck no."

Onyx's green eyes turned dark as Ames opened the door and growled as he squeezed the knob. "Come to die, chaos magician?"

My heart froze and I joined my archdemon, feeling the presence of my guys beside me.

Zyre flicked us all passive glances. "Bad time?" he asked, smirking. "The pack's looking a little thin, Wolfgang. Did something happen today?"

The growl Wolf emitted shook the house as Onyx held him back. "You have three seconds to speak before I let him go," Onyx answered, "and before I join him."

"I wanted to give you one more chance, Blythe," he said, addressing me, still wearing his stupid clown face paint.

Ames gave the phantom a hard shove, and he stepped backward onto the porch. "Don't talk to her. Don't even look at her."

"Oh, I don't want your whore, demon—"

I gasped as Zyre fell backward down Wolf's stairs, struggling to pull himself to a stand as he held his bleeding lip. "My Claimed is the only reason you're still breathing right now," Ames threatened, the sound all Ghost.

The phantom dusted off his blazer. "Then she should know that it doesn't matter what you all are scheming now. It's all set in motion, and you can't stop what's coming and who's coming for you, Reaper. This has been going on for hundreds of years, and he'll have you."

I stepped out onto the porch. "Who?"

Zyre only laughed maniacally. "You know who."

"How about we see you back to your little circus of clowns," Onyx threatened, moving in front of me with Wolf on his tail.

"No need." Zyre stepped back. "I'll see you all again very soon." He tipped his hat, and in a flurry of dark glitter, he was gone.

Wolf roared in anger and my heart dropped. This was how my last night with them would be spent—in the wake of chaos.

"When I first brought her to Fenrir in October, I never wanted her to leave. I should have made her my luna then. No offense, Ames," Wolf lamented softly as I drifted in and out of sleep. They weren't sleeping. Just staying awake and watching me, murmuring quietly. It was so wonderful I could have cried, but instead, I listened.

"You know Ghost," Onyx jeered. "He has to be first."

"I'm glad you came around." Wolf sighed.

I knew my pensive archdemon's sigh as he replied, "Having a heart to heart with a sea captain will do that."

The guys chuckled, and I could hear the smirk in Onyx's voice. "I can't wait to hear about that." He rubbed my feet then. "Isn't she beautiful when she sleeps?"

The guys all agreed, and I buried the warm tears behind my eyes.

What if I failed? What if I never saw them again?

Morning came, and I was fed a hearty breakfast that I forced myself to eat. All I could think about was the faces of ghouls, the shrieks of diphylla, and the lifeless bodies of the dead foxes. Maybe I was an idiot for trying, but I had to. I couldn't not. Onyx and Ames walked with me to meet Nephele on the edge of the forest, at the entrance into the woods.

"Seriously second-guessing this," Ames said, rubbing a nervous hand down my back.

"It's not too late to lock her in a dungeon," Onyx agreed.

I giggled. "Stop. I'm going to be fine."

They stopped my path, each looking like wholly different versions of dark princes. Ames, cool and icy, Onyx with his vampiric fire.

"We've decided you have five days," Ames said lowly. "My hell smoke will follow you as far as it can so I can sense you. If you're not back in five days, we come looking. Phantoms, monsters, and wolves be damned, okay?"

Onyx put his hands on my shoulders, and I felt a surge of calm and optimism invade my senses. A gift from him. "They can't see you. Just follow the path up the mountain and ignore anything you hear or see."

I was sure a chill was trying to slither down my spine, but his empathic gifts blocked it. Looking around, I realized I'd been searching for Wolfgang all morning. "Where's Wolf?"

The guys looked at each other. "He, um… couldn't be here. But told us to give you his love," Onyx replied.

That didn't sound right. But I had no time to question them as the lunas converged at the base of the tree line.

"This is all we know," Nephele stated. "At the top of the mountain, where the horned berries grow, the scents go cold." She draped a hooded cloak around my back. "Red, for courage," she said and placed a basket in my hands. "And flowers and herbs for protection."

Shit, this was getting real.

I took a deep breath, finding the grieving, worried mother in the crowd of wolves. My fear eased then as we locked eyes. "They're coming back with me, I promise." It was a big promise, one I didn't know if I was capable of keeping, but the woman nodded.

The white wolf, Nephele, whispered, "Calliach is our pack's grandmother wolf. She is powerful. She will leave clues. She will call to you if you listen for her. Find our grandmother, Blythe. Find our lost pups. Bring them home."

I gave Ames and Onyx each a tearful kiss and peeled myself out of their hold, my heart breaking as I stepped away. My heart bleeding because Wolfgang wasn't there to say goodbye. And I stepped into the woods, clutching my basket, a hood of red over my ears, and into monster territory.

Through the woods, over the mountain, to grandmother wolf I went.

CHAPTER 28

PAWS WITH CLAWS

> Stars, hide your fires; Let not light see my black and deep desires.
> *William Shakespeare*

Much of my childhood was a blur. There wasn't much I could recall before my mother was murdered. I wasn't an exceptionally talented kid. My grades were subpar, but my imagination was vivid. When my mother wouldn't come home at night, or I was afraid in my room, I'd imagine I was in some fantastical land. That I was lost in some fairy-tale place. It's what I pretended as I walked that day through the woods, following the path that Wolf and I had traveled up to the waterfall. I'd be passing it, which made me happy. Every so often, I'd hear a branch snap, and my heart would drop, but I would keep walking, pretending that it was just a stroll through the woods. And not the truth… which was that I was being hunted.

The first night, I huddled at the chopped trees that Wolf had taken me to when we'd first arrived. It comforted me to know he'd been there. Though he'd gotten us here a lot faster in his wolf form than I'd done on foot. I didn't know anything about camping, but my cloak made for a good blanket, and the jerky from my bag was enough to make me full enough to sleep in a tiny thicket of tree stumps. Soft, almost indiscernible blue fog peppered around me and comforted my worried thoughts.

"Hi, Ghost, I love you, too," I whispered as I drifted off, ignoring the screeching sounds in the brush beyond. My boys were worried, and I was, too. But in the same breath, it was time. I'd been helpless and hiding, a kite floating by the string of their strength and whims, adrift in this realm that was now my home. Wolf's arms had always been the ones I'd found myself tied up in. He'd always protected me and expected nothing in return. He'd offered me his home, his people, without knowing me for longer than a day. And I was doing this for him, for the Halloween Boys, for Fenrir.

The next day, I found the waterfall just as dusk was sailing away, taking with it the remnants of colors and whistles of the water spirits. It made me smile to think that this magical light show happened with or without any viewers. Or maybe her performance was just for herself and the trees. I filled up my canteen and splashed my face with cold water as the multicolored lights flicked and faded like rainbow fireflies ascending into the pointed pines. When I cupped water in my palms for the second time, the lights went out, as if shut off completely, and something red glimmered in the reflection of my hands. When I looked up, nothing was there, but the feeling of being watched sank in my gut like a heavy stone.

I awoke with the smell of smoke and fire pervasive in my nose, which was odd, because I hadn't built a fire the night before, being too cautious of the sensation of eyes on me. It was an effort to move away from the waterfall into unknown territory, to the base of the mountain I had to climb. Leaving behind what I knew, my comfort, my protectors. The pathway encircled the mountain, and the trail was worn with twisted tree roots and dotted with pink flower confetti from blooming redbud trees. Every so often, the path would widen into an overlook, and I would stop and look out over Fenrir and Ash Grove and be comforted. Maybe this would work as well as the lunas and I hoped it would. Being invisible had brought me this far without much to speak of.

And then at dawn, as I was petting the soft moss on a boulder, a blood-curdling screech rang out. The smell of rotten eggs panicked my senses as I ducked behind the rock, inching into the tiny space between it and the mountain. The ghouls were silent, but the diphylla that seemed to follow them around were not. They gurgled and clicked as the rustle of them and the smell of the ghouls approached. *Please, just be passing through,* I chanted in my mind. *Keep walking, keep walking.* I held my breath as their shadows blocked the remaining sunlight. Why had they stopped?

The dirt kicked up again, and the huffs of the diphylla moved forward, and I let out an exhale at their passing. I dared to slowly peek out around the green moss and—

Something sharp grabbed my ankle. My scream shook through me as the ghoul hissed, its grip cold, like it wasn't a living thing. "I have you now, Blythe." It hissed my name, pulling and dragging me across the dirt path while two others surrounded us. "Master will be pleased."

I struggled against it when something pricked my calf, stinging like a viper bite, invading my system with poison, calling to my consciousness, and sinking me into blackness, into sleep. I was going to die.

CHAPTER 29
Wolf

PETER LOST WENDY

> I wish you to know you have been the last dream of
> my soul.
> *Charles Dickens*

Heaviness weighed down my shoulders. My grandfather's pecan bars sugared my tongue. Sometimes the old tastes or smells of when I was a pup would wake me up, leaving behind some lesson hidden between two half-awake memories. He'd died long ago, but his legacy as an elder carried on. If our elder grandfathers and grandmothers were indeed locked away, and Blythe was the one to free them, her journey was noble and righteous, and I was proud to call her mine. But I didn't give a shit about the lunas or Fenrir or wolf politics at the moment. I'd steal her away like Onyx had. Whisk her to safety. But I knew the feeling of my hybrid lover's touch as my emotions steadied, my head leveled, and I slept.

They'd done what I'd asked them to do. As the full moon approached, as the alpha raged like a destructive wildfire in my chest, raging for his mate, I rattled my chains in the hollow space.

Sniffing, I knew where I was instantly, and instantly regretted putting Ghost in charge of chaining my beast.

Then I met the glowing green eyes in the corner. "You didn't think I'd leave you down here all alone, did you?"

"A crypt?" I questioned, sniffing again and realizing there was something protruding over my nose and mouth.

"So very cliché of Ghost, isn't it? I said the same. But yes, my love, and the mask was my idea. I'm the only one allowed to bite our girl. You know that," Onyx drawled, though there was pain behind his eyes. "I do hate this. All of it."

"Me, too," I hung my head, leaning against the shackles that secured my wrists to the high ceiling of the underground grave. "But I'm a threat to her safety."

Onyx shrugged. "We don't know that yet. But if you're more comfortable this way, I'll consent to your demands."

"How do you know you won't hurt her when you drink from her? How does Ghost know he won't rip her apart as an archdemon?"

My vampire slowly walked over and took the bars of my muzzle with both hands. "We've made friends with our monsters, Wolf. It's your turn to do the same. It doesn't diminish your goodness, love. Nothing could ever do that."

I huffed. "What goodness? She's—" I inhaled sharply. "Oh, fuck, she's gone? I didn't say goodbye. How long have I been out like this?"

"A few days. The moon is full"—he looked at his watch—"tonight or tomorrow. I'm bad at reading the stars."

I pulled against my binding in a fury, but they didn't budge. "Let me out," I yelled. "I'm going to go get her now."

"Ghost has been watching her with his smoke. She's almost up the mountain. She's so close to finding the answer to all this shit. Trust me, one sign of danger, and we're all there."

"No," I growled. "This isn't right. Something isn't right. I can smell it."

Onyx gave my exposed chest a small kiss. "I'll check on you after the full moon, after the alpha goes back to sleep. Try to rest. We've got everything covered, okay?"

My scream of fury shook the graves and rattled the spirits. Even the damned hushed at my outraged cries. Something wasn't right, but I couldn't articulate it. Blythe was in danger. She needed me.

No, she needs me. She needs us like this, my alpha answered from deep within me. He was lying. He had to be. I couldn't allow that part of me to take control. My alpha didn't understand that Blythe wasn't a wolf. She was breakable, delicate, and small. Harm would not come to her again because of my crazed werewolf form. But I kept feeling his pull as night crept onward, as the moon rose, as my hands elongated and sharped with claws. I watched, enraptured, as my forearms widened and covered in my wolf's fur. I grew so tall I wasn't hanging from the chains on the ceiling anymore. I was hunched under it… and my maw… it filled the muzzle to a tight extreme. My fangs gnawed at the metal bars.

But could I do what Onyx and Ghost had done? Could I trust the monster inside me with the love of my life? Was that a risk I could make, unleashing him and setting him loose?

As the moon poured in through the bars of my enclosure, a forlorn howl shattered through me, searching for the answer.

CHAPTER 30

Blythe

RED OR DEAD

I don't know why that, on that last breath before plunging into darkness, I hoped to meet the devil in my dreams. He'd always implied that I called him to me, that I'd found him in my sleep, but when only black and uncertainty greeted me, I decided then that the devil was a liar. And no one was coming to save me.

A bitter smoke smell invaded my nose again. So strong, too strong. When I opened my eyes, I was lying near a small campfire and someone was stoking the blaze. He was a blur of red and the source of the bitter smell. Did he smell particularly strong, or was it something in me? Was this how wolves experienced this sense?

Sitting up, I held my pounding head. "Easy there," he cooed. "Ghoul poison takes a while to wear off. It's basically the worst hangover of your life if you survive it. Most don't. You're lucky he didn't take your skin."

As the man blurred into focus, I recognized him, but realized I'd never actually spoken to him. "Carmine?" I asked, my throat scratchy.

"Never thought you paid attention to me," he answered, passing me a water canteen. "You're far too important to converse with the likes of a lower wolven."

When I reached for the water, my wrists tugged together and my chest tightened. I tried to stand, but my ankles were tied, too. "What the hell?"

He squatted next to me and splashed the liquid roughly against my lips. I was angry at my need to accept it, though in that moment, I shouldn't have accepted anything from the traitor.

He drawled, "I considered pretending, you know, to come up here and be your friend. But, you see, I don't underestimate you like your little boyfriends do. No, I'm not so easily fooled." He rubbed his red beard.

"And how do I play into your master plan as you betray your pack, Carmine?" I asked, searching my brain for a plan of escape. The mountain pass was narrow, but it opened to another overlook soon. If I could get away somehow, I could lose him.

He chuckled darkly. "Oh, you still haven't figured it out? I'm even better than I thought. But that's what actual hard work and training gets you. None of this being spoon-fed by a gang of assholes who never worked a day in their life."

A menacing voice purred through my mind, making my ears ring. *Not all fights are brawn, dear girl. Not all battles are that of power or even magic. More often than not, pure nerve and a calm mind will do more for you than your tricks.* My heart leapt at hearing the devil. Maybe he was around after all.

And then it all made sense. How the ghouls always made it into Fenrir, the pups going missing while Carmine was on call, him finding me now and the chaos magician showing up right before I left on this journey. The red wolf… the ace of spades.

"Zyre," I breathed.

He smirked. "See? I knew you were smarter than you look.

And the company you keep. A newly formed alpha's mind is so moldable, so gullible and easy to play with. He believed me to be one of his pack immediately."

A plan began to form, but I'd have to be careful. Channeling every powerful woman I'd ever met, I thought of Ezmerelda and her sensuous charm that got her everything she wanted. I thought of Queen Cassiopeia and her soft subtlety, the lunas of Fenrir with their loyal vigor, and the witches with their quick knowledge and intelligence. I could be a bit of all of them, I thought, and any one of them alone was more than the dark phantom would ever be.

"I'm glad you finally caught up," I breathed. "We could have had this out at the waterfall, but you were too shy to come out and play."

He raised a skeptical eyebrow and sat cross-legged, pulling out a deck of cards. "Come again?"

I tilted my head. "Why do you think I worked so hard to get them to let me off my leash? If I'm stolen away, they'll just hunt me down forever, like you said, tearing through time and space to get me back." I shrugged. "But if I leave on my own, what can they do? They'll move on. Like you said, I'm not that special apart from my ambiguous abilities."

Zyre, in the body of a burly, redheaded man, paused mid-shuffle. "You're fucking with me, aren't you?"

"Where do I have the most opportunity, Zyre? Stuck in Ash Grove? Granted, having great sex. Or following you to your master and learning what I can really do with my reaper powers? I need a teacher."

His gaze locked on mine. "Everyone needs a teacher. We're nothing without them."

"Duh, why do you think the wolves are so focused on getting their elders back? But I don't have one, because there aren't reapers just lying around. But you found a teacher, didn't you? You did it the hard way."

He puffed up a bit and nodded, shuffling his cards again. "I'm not as old as the Halloween Boys. No, I went to my first circus as a boy in nineteen forty-three. Saw the phantoms there, knew what they were doing wasn't natural, wasn't of this world. Those chaos magicians used their gift for tricks and money, but I knew I could use it for so much more."

I lay back, putting my hands behind my head, feigning nonchalance like Onyx so often did. A mask of his, I'd learned, a really effective one. "Well, have fun carrying me to your master. I can't wait to meet him and get this show started. Though, I sort of wanted to meet the elders first, but whatever. It doesn't really matter."

"I don't particularly want to carry you on my back as a dirty fucking wolf, and I don't want to exhaust my magic by knocking you out either. Not when those abhorrent creatures in the woods would snap me in half to get to you. They don't care that we're on the same fucking team. If I let you go, how do I know you won't run away?"

"You don't, I guess. But where am I running to on a mountaintop with those monsters everywhere?"

"Ah, they're stupid. They follow orders once and always, no matter if you try to tell them differently. He sent them after you a long time ago."

"He who?"

Suddenly, he was leaning over me with a knife. I closed my eyes and braced for its sting when my arms went slack. And then my ankles. "You'll see." He smiled. "Quiet, silent type of guy, but he's the most powerful fucking dude you'll ever meet."

Trying to contain my satisfaction, I hugged my knees and took another sip from the canteen on the ground. "Cool," I responded. "Where to?"

"Same direction you're already going. There's a portal at the top. You'll see. More magic than Ash Grove and Fenrir and Belladonia combined."

Running made no sense. And launching some sort of half-baked attack against him didn't either. He wasn't ancient, but he was still old and twisted up in dark magic. He was like me, stronger than he let on. And he'd been planning this for a while. But regardless, like I was learning from my time on this side of monsterhood, he was still a male… and men were gullible.

So I slept next to my enemy that night, pretending nothing was wrong, pretending I was as evil as he was. I didn't dare make a move, because regardless of my ropes being cut, I was still locked beneath his power of wit. I'd wait and pretend to sleep as my own battle plans played in my mind.

I WOKE WITH A START, seeing a huge red wolf peering at me. He was gruffer and not nearly as muscular as Wolf in his shifted form, but I didn't let on that anything was amiss. We were going in the same direction anyway. I would figure out a way to ditch him once I made it to the top. I was under no delusion that Zyre couldn't kill me in whatever form he wanted, so I'd have to keep playing the game with him in the meantime.

Suddenly, the red wolf turned around, sniffing, looking to me and then sniffing the air. "What is it?"

He snarled over my shoulder as four ghouls and a host of diphylla behind them ascended the trail. I exhaled, not having to feign my true irritation. "I'm invisible; you're not. They smelled you," I said, backing away. He nipped at my ankles, as if to tell me not to run. "What else am I supposed to do?" I asked him. "Stand and get eaten by your stupid ghouls?"

Zyre in wolf form lunged at the ghouls. I guessed they were easier to defeat as a beast than a magic-man. But his form was nothing like the wolves of Fenrir. He wasn't canine. He hadn't trained. And as two focused on him, two more came for me, hissing my name. "Shit." I backed away, almost tripping on my cloak.

Looking around for anything, any help or escape route, I met the wide gaze of brown eyes. Two wooden fingers gestured me forward up the trail as they whistled an upbeat tune. I guessed following a wooden forest spirit was my best option, and, turning on my heel, I raced after it. Snarls and hisses snapped behind me as I rounded the corner, wincing, knowing I was one pierce of their talons away from plunging into disorientation again. But when I opened my eyes, despite the sunny morning hour, it was milky twilight again. The trail opened up to an overlook washed in violet, with sparkling grays and bobbing turquoise flowers. It was like the human world, only the color and feeling of it were so different. Odd. It couldn't be more different, but the atmosphere almost reminded me of Hallows Fest. Something jumped up and down, revealing itself and then disappearing under tall grass and cattail leaves.

"Thank you," I told the spirit. "Do you know where the wolves are? Are they near here?"

The creature made me yelp as it appeared on my shoe, cocking its head at an odd angle. It shrugged. "I told you your journey would be easier on this side of the veil."

"Is this the spirit world?" I asked, looking around. It was like being underwater and in the clouds at the same time.

When it didn't answer, I remembered what the luna had told me about forest spirits. I reached around for my bag and pulled out a red apple, then knelt before the misshapen little tree sprite. "Would you like some fruit?"

Its eyes widened as it snatched it from my grip. "The wolves got caught behind the veil. Some fell in. Some were brought here, like the puppies."

"Where?"

It took a bite of the apple, shocking me with its hidden pointed teeth. They let the juice drip down their chin. "Just up there. In the hawthorn tree of many mothers. I'll take you, and we can be friends again now."

I nodded, thankful for the lunas, thankful for the apple and for this veil of protection. It was beautiful here, and little petals of dandelions floated past my nose as we trekked up to an enormous tree covered in red berries. But it wasn't just one tree. It was several. There were maybe a dozen separate trees, all joined together at the base. The spirit appeared, hanging from a branch. "Jump inside the water," it instructed.

I stepped up onto a root and looked into the middle of the circle formation. Sure enough, there was a tiny bath of sorts of glowing gold water. Fear and awareness prickled my neck. What would happen if I obeyed and jumped in? Spirits were generally friendly but also tricky… this could all be one big trick…

And then I heard a cry that shook me to my core. A cry I never wanted to hear. The howl of a wolf that shouldn't be here. Leaving the tree, I sprinted back the way I came, seeing the veil thin to a point where I could make out blurry images on the other side. An enormous half wolf, half man stood, throwing ghouls off his back. He grabbed the red wolf that attacked him and dislocated his shoulder with a snap as he yowled in pain, and a flurry of glitter exploded. The werewolf sniffed. And he shouldn't have been able to—how could he have?—but he did. He smelled me, and his feral amber gaze locked with mine, though his maw was covered in a muzzle. All of a sudden, his claws plunged into the veil and he howled, using all his might to tear into it, creating a slit where sunlight poured through. When I'd first arrived in Fenrir, I'd run from him, his wild beast scaring me. But this time, I ran toward him, holding on to his wrists. "Wolfgang, I'm here," I assured him.

My touch was all he needed, and with another howl, he peeled back the veil and jumped inside with me. The shards rippled closed behind him, locking out the world. "Blythe," he said, out of breath, scarred and on all fours. But then he stood, so tall and long. The body of a man but the face of a beast. This was the alpha, the werewolf, the monster inside my man… and for some reason, there were shackles around his wrists and a muzzle on his maw.

I took a tentative step forward, reaching out a hand. "Wolfgang?" I asked.

His focus shot up, blazing into me with his amber gaze as he growled, "I'm going to eat you now."

CHAPTER 31

Alpha Wolf

ALL THE BETTER

I'd found her. I'd been set free, and I'd found her. It was easy. She was my moon. I followed my moon, my luna. And the filth that hunted her, the betrayer, the stench of monster scum that wanted her. I'd ripped them apart with my hands. Even without my teeth, they were nothing but dead things. Then I sensed her. She was there but not, and I'd found my claws strong enough to tear apart the fabrics of our realms and propel myself into hers. And there she was, looking afraid but smelling like sex, like she was ovulating under the full moon, just for me, waiting for my monster cock. Before she could run, I pounced on her, pinning her beneath me in the same way I'd captured her in the graveyard when we'd first been brought back to Ash Grove.

"Your fangs." She shuddered under me. "My, what big teeth you have."

"All the better to eat you with, my dear," I growled in my alpha's baritone. I licked her collarbone, tasting the dirt on her skin and the salty sweat beneath, dragging my long tongue up her neck to lap at her jaw. She shivered beneath me, and her breathing picked up as her fingers roamed through the fur on my chest.

"Are you ready for the big bad wolf?" I nudged my enormous length against her stomach, and she swallowed in apprehension. Despite her fear, she ran her fingers down the metal of my muzzle, finding the leather hooks and unfastening them. She tossed it aside in an act of acceptance, of bravery. My little luna was ready for me. She lay in the grass. The purple tint of beyond the veil darkened her features. Her hair was splayed out atop her red cloak. My own Little Red Riding Hood for my enjoyment, my tasting, my eating. My alpha had searched and found her, hunted his prey. But beneath him, at his core, I found the Fenrir wolf shifter who'd sniffed out the flowers planted by his mate and returned with the blooms worthy of his luna, deserving of Laverna and spring. Then, beneath the smell of my wolven, was a man. I inhaled as the beast, scenting the canine within me and sensing the man. The humble, good-seeking servant who recognized his power in kneeling before the greatness around him. The man in me wasn't as weak as I thought. He was strong. So strong he'd tamed the beasts inside and won the love of darkness in the form of a woman. The man, the beast, the merging of both, and the devotion to Death herself.

I wouldn't hurt her. We wouldn't hurt her. But we would certainly make her scream and die a little death of pleasure under her werewolf. We could swallow her whole, man, beast, and the joining of the two. She tilted her chin and nuzzled against my maw as her hands roamed my shoulders, down to squeeze my biceps and forearms. Larger, mightier than even my human form.

"What big hands you have," she whispered.

I lifted a black claw-tipped palm and ran it slowly over her breast. "All the better to touch you with."

Her breathing hitched as my claw circled her nipple, making it stand at attention.

Her gaze roamed to my eyes, and she smiled, seeing Wolfgang glowing in their amber. She pulled at one of my ears. "What big ears you have."

"All the better to hear you moan for me," I growled, pulling back my hips and lining the head of my cock up with her wet slit. Her mouth fell open in a pant of want, and she moved her touch down my abdomen and to my length. When she grabbed it in two hands, I let her explore for a moment, her eyes wide in wonder at the size and girth my shifted form afforded.

"What a big cock you have," she whimpered. I reached down, hooking a claw inside her panties and ripping them swiftly.

"All the better to fuck you with." My grit turned half howl as I plunged into her depths. She screamed, her walls tightening in protest at my thick intrusion. Fuck, she hugged me just right, and I buried myself to the hilt as she wiggled, her body searching for room to take me in.

Maybe my size and her strain pulled her to me, or maybe she bucked her hips with every retreat of mine. Each slam back into her elicited another lovely moan of pleasure, and she wrapped her arms around me, affording me the access I wanted to her neck.

As I pummeled in and out, I wrapped my maw around her throat and squeezed the sides, controlling every breath in and out. My teeth sank in just enough to bruise, just enough so she couldn't move, couldn't escape my breeding. Because I would breed her. I'd fill her with my cum so deep she'd never escape me. My cum would infiltrate her and make her a wolf, too. At least in spirit she was now. My luna, my brave Little Red Riding Hood fucking her big bad wolf. "You take me so good, little one," I ground out as my tongue licked at her neck.

"Wolfgang, oh my god." She moaned as I fucked her slow and hard, somehow inching deeper into her with each thrust.

The veil shimmered with orbs of color, as if the realm beyond itself was pleased by our love, our passion, our celebration of the land and the spirit would. Our festival of life and death contained within our passion. I fucked Blythe with a vigor I'd never known, and she came with a thunderous cry as I roared my release into her at the same moment. Her walls milked me as I flooded her with my seed, my knot growing at the base of where our bodies connected, keeping it in place. She pushed against my chest and whimpered at the intrusion within her sensitive cunt.

My werewolf only growled and tightened his grip on her neck. She wasn't escaping this. "You'll hold on to every drop and keep me in your womb forever. Do you understand?"

With breathless whines, she arched her back and nodded, pushing herself closer to me in a *yes* from her body to mine. She wanted it, too. Needed it. Needed my essence inside of her, to grow, to live on, to create new life and usher in a new soul. Not a physical one, but a soul connection of new life, the heart of Laverna, the core of breeding. Love and sex in their truest form created life, life for her, life for me, and a divine combination of us both.

When the violet hues slowed their dance around us and the grass hushed its rustle, I slowly unhooked my bite and allowed my knot to slide from her. I rose to my knees, always on my knees for her, my luna. She joined me and wrapped around me in the hug. The same hug from October, from February, the same hug I'd be blessed with until the end of time and then after.

"I love you, Wolf," she whispered.

"I love you," I responded, not even knowing my alpha could utter those words. But he did. "I am your lowly wolf. You are my moon. And I will chase after your light forever."

CHAPTER 32

Blythe

ACE OF SPADES

> Some days I am more wolf than woman, and I am
> still learning how to stop apologizing for my wild.
> *Nikita Gill*

We stayed tied together for moments that were suspended in time. He inhaled the scent of my hair and cocooned me under his massive frame. Once I caught my breath, I wiggled and shoved against him. "Wolf, I have to go. I think I know where to find the missing wolves." I ran my fingers over his chest and down his arms until he pulled out of me. Helping me stand, he pulled my red hood over my head.

"Little Red Riding Hood," he said lowly, in a voice that was entirely Wolf's but different, older. This was him as the alpha, as the werewolf, and I liked him like this. It suited him. As I looked up at him and admired his form, the merging of two, a man and a beast, I marveled at how I'd transformed, too, letting my own wolf come out to play. Under the full moon, I'd merged two parts of myself, too. The girl and the reaper… or I was about to, at least.

We smelled it at the same time, the overwhelming and pungent aroma of smoke. Silver glitter erupted as a silver knife plunged into Wolf's side. I screamed as he turned around with a roar, grabbing Zyre by the throat as ghouls and diphyllas tore at the entrance through the veil, sliding in and jumping at my werewolf. I steadied myself to help, to fight, to do anything, but Wolf locked his stare with mine.

"Run," he demanded.

But I wasn't running home, and I didn't think he was asking me to. My sprints weren't that of a frightened little girl. They were that of a brave luna wolf. I knew what I had to do. Taking off and running as fast as I could, I slammed into the connected hawthorn trees. The tree sprite was nowhere to be found. It didn't matter. I was jumping in regardless.

I climbed up the gnarly knobs as sounds of shrieks and roars and the combustion of chaos magic made me cringe and worry for Wolf. But I could finally help him, or I could find those that could. If I was right about where they were trapped. Steady, I lowered a foot into the glistening gold water that pooled between the trees and was shocked to find it wasn't a wet feeling. It simply felt like cool air. Not feeling the bottom, I took a deep breath. The hissing and screams were fast approaching me now. With a yank, I untied the ribbon around my neck and inched my other foot in, letting go and falling. My red cloak floated to the ground behind me, dirty, worn, and tattered. Little Red Riding Hood had been devoured by a wolf. And that wolf was me.

WHEN I MADE contact with something solid, I realized I was in a tunnel of sorts and had to crawl toward the light. How befitting for Death to be crawling toward a tunnel of light, I thought. Devil was surely somewhere mocking me as he sipped a scotch. As the exit grew larger, I reached the opening and walked out into bright, golden light. The merriment of giggles reached my ears and confused me. I never knew what to expect anymore, but happiness was the last thing on my mind. Suddenly, two sets of arms wrapped around my knees. "Hi!" They giggled. "You found us.

Now it's your turn to play hide and seek," the little girl from Fenrir said. "The willow spirit told us you were great at hide and seek."

My heart gripped as I dropped to my knees and hugged the missing pups. "You guys are all right," I said, more to myself than anymore. "What do you mean the willow spirit?"

The little girl laughed and pulled away. "You know, the funny little wooden guy!"

My little wood spirit was the willow? How... But I didn't have time to marvel. A group of women approached me. The light caught around them like moonbeams and sunshine all at once as the oldest woman approached me. "Grandmother wolf?" I asked. "Calliach?"

She smiled a wrinkled smile. "I'm glad to see you, Death. Shall we move on now?"

The other lunas, some human, some wolves, looked to her and me, waiting for my answer. Until I realized what she was asking and shook my head. "No, no, not yet. I'm taking you back. All of you. Fenrir needs you. Wolf needs you—we all need you."

Calliach smiled. "Then so be it. We've visited this place for long enough. You know, many wolves can move between the realms with ease, though every now and then, we get stuck and need a little help to cross back over. So is the story of our Wolfgang's alpha form." Winking at me, she looked over my shoulder toward the way I came, and her gray brows furrowed in concern. "I believe something is asking for your attention there. Perhaps have a look before we depart."

When I turned, it was the bundle of hawthorn trees again, but they had turned black, and the water in the middle glowed red. Fear rippled through me as I slowly touched it and looked into the pond. And then images invaded my mind as the tide rippled and fear squeezed my throat.

I was standing in the center of Ash Grove as flames and ash burned around me. People were screaming and sobbing. I looked around, feeling panic. The images were all moving so fast. All I wanted to do was find the guys. And then I saw my boys. Each of their beautiful faces. My Ghost, Dragon, and Wolf... and they were lying on the ground, lifeless,—dead.

As I gasped in horror and fell to my knees, the image flashed, and I was in a white room, one I recognized from Halloween. An empty throne sat before me, and I was standing before it. When I turned around, I realized I wasn't alone. Three women stood, assessing me, each looking regal and wild and powerful.

One shrouded in dark purple shadow smiled behind her black gaze. "Mortala, so nice to see you."

"Who—who are you guys?"

One with long wavy blond hair that trailed behind her like a train giggled. It sounding like a harp. She reminded me of Onyx's mother. "Absolutely not **guys.***"*

The third woman didn't speak, only smiled softly.

The one in purple light spoke. "We think there's much for you to learn before you take your seat there, and we'd like to help you."

Seeing the elders, being immersed in Fenrir with the lunas, and even my conversations with Zyre had led me to the same conclusion they were proposing. They were right. I needed a teacher. "I need the help. And my mates need your help. What I just saw—" I stumbled over the words. "It was fire to our home, and they were dead... I can't let that happen. How do I save them? How do I keep that vision from becoming reality?"

The blond one tilted her head. "We can show you how to be what you are, but you have to come to us. You have to go to him."

"Him?" I asked.

The one in purple looked over her shoulder, as if she could see something I couldn't. "The ruler of the underworld, of course. He is your winter. You are his spring. Together you shall bring about a glorious autumn."

I held my head, feeling desperate for more guidance as they gradually disappeared. "And he can help keep them safe? He can help me save the Halloween Boys?"

The urge to cry and scream and demand they stay overtook me as the vision faded. Then the tree was white again, and I was surrounded by lunas and elders. I steeled my shaking knees and forced myself to remember what was happening now. Not the feeling of the guys' lifeless bodies on the ground. The foreboding and heavy emotion of impending despair took my breath away.

"This way," I barely managed a whisper.

I waited until every luna, elder, and pup had passed through the pond in the middle of the trees. As I stood alone on the other side, the place of bright light, I inhaled deeply, as if I could swallow and absorb some of this realm's light. Then I pushed the darkness from my mind for Wolf, for Fenrir, for the boys. Clearly, more dangers, more questions, still loomed beyond my grasp. But I'd have to settle that another time. Resting my forehead against the smooth bark of the tree and gathering myself for a moment, I let go and dropped into the mist behind them.

As fog swirled around me, the guttural and haunting sounds of wolves echoed through the atmosphere. A smile tugged at the corner of my lips at the music of war cries of the warrior women. The mother wolves, the elders, the lunas, blessed me. Then a howl shuddered around me, with dozens of answering howls answering it. My werewolf was okay. They were winning. Fenrir was back at last.

Eager to see them, I reached the opening where dull light awaited. When I came out the other side, though, I wasn't on the overlook anymore. Instead, I stepped into a familiar round room. Standing in the center was Zyre. Only this time, he didn't look at me as confidently as he had last time. It was then I realized this was *my* room. I had called him here. All this time, this space hadn't been an accident. It had been mine somehow. The phantom had played me before, like a game of cards. But he wouldn't play me again.

My anger, the visions of the guys in the fire, staggered through my mind. The pain of Fenrir roiled in my veins as I addressed him. "You've hurt people I love. You've stolen from Fenrir, lied and deceived them. You let children be taken. You attacked my men and you burned one of their houses down."

"We're both liars, it would seem," he breathed, out of breath.

I'd hoped Wolf had killed him. Now I was happy he hadn't. "So what now? Kill me? Fine. Go ahead, but it doesn't change your fate. You're playing into his hand whether you realize it or not. And my master is patient. If he doesn't have you now, it's because it's not time."

"I'll deal with your master next. For now…" I looked around the circular gray room of nothingness. "So different from a circus in here, isn't it? No color, no warmth, no fun… no distractions. What was it you told me? That the only unforgivable sin is being boring, isn't that right? "

Zyre met my gaze in a slight panic.

"How about you wait here for me until I need to talk to you again?" I smiled. "Oh, and I think you're wrong about something else. I'm Death. *I'm* the ace of spades, not you."

He screamed in agony when I let go of the interaction and let him and the room dim away… There were doors stretched out before me, doors like in Belladonia, and I spotted the ones left ajar and closed them tight. Locking in the monsters and clicking back to locks that kept the vampire city's enchantments in place. When I reached the end of the white hallway, my feet landed in soft, wet grass again. I breathed in the aroma of meat and fire, the gorgeous chorus of children laughing and families being reunited. Ash Grove, Fenrir, my boys… I was home again.

CHAPTER 33

Wolf

LAVERNA

If I were the moon, I'd like you to be my night.
Alexandra Vasiliu

The nectar of sweet reunions wafted heavy in the spring Fenrir air. Lunas and elders hugged my neck, and missing pups, reunited with family, played at my feet. The tears I'd been holding back, tears of sorrow and loss, fell and transformed like a June rain. Washing away the grit of winter and ushering forth the blessings and gratitude of warmer days, of bounty, of a community of love.

Our Laverna pole was resurrected in the center of our commune and dripping in vines and flowers. Children danced around it, wrapping it in ribbons and singing old songs of the wolven. Everything was falling back in order, as if no time had passed at all. As if our lunas and elders had merely taken a vacation behind the veil. The adolescent wolves prepared the feast without being asked and served the elders without my direction. The lunas fell back into their patrol. Though, now, with the portals closed and the chaos magic spells broken, there wouldn't be more monsters flooding our forests, and the ghouls would fear us again.

Music thrummed, and I smiled as Onyx played guitar while

Ames and Blythe twirled. She was barefoot and laughing, wearing a shade of pink on her lips I knew was just for me. Before I could join them, I had business to attend to with the other wolves. A fellow sol and I exchanged glances of happiness as we shifted and took off into the woods. Sniffing, seeking. Not for hunt or kills, not for monsters and blood—for flowers, for love, for the bulbs planted by our mates.

I came across a mossy clearing with the lush and soft green grass I'd always loved to roll in. And in the middle of the circle bloomed the finest glowing moon flowers I'd ever seen. My heart warmed. They were perfect for her, and she'd planted them just for me, for me to find. Blythe would always be mine to find, tend, water, and celebrate.

Taking them in my maw, a small voice not of this world said above me, "You're a good wolf." It was the wooden little tree sprite. It wasn't the first time a fairy had spoken to me in this form, but it had been some time.

I looked up to the trees, wagging my tail. "Thank you," I replied, knowing compliments from fairy folk were hard to come by.

It whistled a tune and strung a melody together as I padded off, but the lyrics stopped me in my tracks. *"He's a good wolf who made a deal with a bad devil. Yes he is,"* the spirit chimed and laughed.

I looked over my shoulder, feeling guilt creep into my joy like a dense fog, but the spirit was gone. Snorting, I shook my head and resumed my mission. I'd handle that ill-fated bargain later... Or never, I hoped.

As I fiddled with the flowers and the branches, the guys and Blythe sat next to me.

"What are you working on?" Blythe asked.

I turned my shoulder to her. "Don't look. You'll see."

Nephele stood, adorned in flowers and looking light and happy for once. She deserved it. Fenrir would not be standing without her. She'd make a wonderful elder someday, and I was proud to lead this pack alongside her. The pups laughed as Nephele acted out a story. She told them one more tale before bedtime and the adult activities could begin…

"As the lunas and elders had emerged from the tree, bringing the lost pups with them, they'd attacked the ghouls and vampire monsters—destroying them in one swoop of power."

The pups cheered and pounced at each other, and I couldn't stop my chuckle at the sight.

"And the great deceiver, the wolf in disguise, was outed by our friend the archdemon—and our alpha broke through his chains to capture him."

Blythe looked to me with wide eyes. I shrugged. It was true.

Nephele continued, picking up a stick. "Our first alpha sol in centuries emerged, clawing through realms for his mate and his pack. He grabbed the chaos pretender and snapped his neck." She broke the stick for dramatic effect, and the pups cheered. Nephele and I exchanged a warm moment. We'd done it.

Blythe tugged my sleeve as I finished up my floral creation. "Zyre is dead?" she asked.

"Ghost sorted it out not long after you left and Carmine disappeared after you. Though his hell smoke did a good job of throwing him off your trail. I freaked when Onyx told me. Broke free and tracked him up the mountain."

"Wait," she clarified. "You killed him? Are you positive?"

"His neck snapped the same as the branch up there." I pointed. "So yes, I'm sure. Why?"

She hummed. "No reason…"

Onyx chimed in, still picking the guitar strings. "Old phantom clown might have thought he was smart, but he believed human fairy tales about werewolves and vampires." He wiggled his bejeweled fingers. "Silver doesn't hurt us. Though it does make me look quite handsome."

Blythe giggled and shoved the vampire hybrid as Ghost twirled a lock of her hair lazily in his fingers, watching the fire contentedly. "I should have figured out what Carmine was sooner, but at least the bastard is dead. Who his master is, however, remains a mystery."

Blythe's smile faltered.

"It's finished." I grinned, showing her my work and delighting in the way her face lit up instantly.

"Wolf." She beamed as I placed it on her head.

"Like it? We find the flowers our luna mate plants and make her these. Crowns for our queens."

"You made me a flower crown." She giggled. "I love it so much… I love you so much."

The squeaking of hinges on doors and the giddiness fading alerted me to the pups being put to bed. Fireflies appeared, then, dotting and dancing along the grass, a golden yellow to the fire's scarlet ember. "Now's time for the real celebration of Laverna," I whispered to my mate. "All of us," I added, meeting Ames's and Onyx's hungry gazes. They would have let me have her to myself tonight, and I loved them for that, but I wanted them, too. Loved them, too. Hell, Onyx and Ames were my mates as much as Blythe was.

Onyx gently eased her dress straps over her shoulders, pushing her dress below her breasts, freeing them to the night sky and for me. "My belladonna, my deadly flower," he sighed in her ear.

"My stunning little ghost," Ames answered beside us.

She lay back against his chest. "Here? Out in the open?"

Ames inched around her and ran a hand down her inner thigh. "Look around, little ghost. All the cool kids are doing it."

She took in her surroundings, and her face flushed with the color of roses. Lunas, sols, and stellas, in all different groups and pairings, were in various stages of sensual celebration.

Blythe let out a breath as Ames's hand found her center and caressed her sex gently. "I wouldn't want to be the one stopping you guys from being the cool kids," she half joked, half whimpered.

Without warning, Onyx bit her neck, and she cried out. Ames

inserted two fingers and moved his fist to the side, allowing me my tasting.

"Ah, yes, my feast," I growled, dipping between her knees. "This is mine tonight." I groaned, running my tongue over her clit. "Want some?" I asked Ames as he watched her hips move against us.

"I do," he purred, moving his head toward me. I caught his lips with mine and darted my tongue into his wanting mouth. He groaned, flicking his forked tongue over mine, lapping up the taste of her and me. "You two are delicious together," he purred. "Like warm honeycomb."

My alpha agreed and let out a howl before uniting my lips to Blythe's cunt once more. Around us, a chorus of howls answered, dripping with bliss and promise under the moon and stars of our Laverna celebration. Her first orgasm of the night answered. The guys and I exchanged glances, sizing up just how we'd take her. How would we share our love tonight, and what would we do to make her scream, make her pant and moan? How could we spend every ounce of energy she had and then leave her ragged and full of our cum? Oh, the possibilities were endless. And now that my beast was free, I was content to leave him untamed and wild—and let the werewolf have her in any way he wanted, whenever he wanted. Because she was mine, they were mine. Everything that existed below the goddamn sky was mine. I was a man, an animal, a monster—and I'd offer all of it for her, for my boys, for my luna. She was my moon, and I'd spend forever howling my devotion at her in the most sincere form of goddess worship. Her whispers in the woods called to me, her crashing waterfall of depth, every bright color of her would enrapture me for the rest of my now too-short life.

"*My luna, my moon.*" I breathed another prayer to her, and her body answered.

AND THEY LIVED HAPPILY EVER AFTER… until…

CHAPTER 34

Blythe

MOTHER WOLF

Dr Clarissa Pinkola Estés

In the days that followed the Laverna blessing at Fenrir, I twirled in flower meadows with pups and laughed with the lunas, retiring to bed at night to tangle in my men. God, this place, this time, was surreal in its idyllic beauty and promise. Wolf had asked to meet me by the waterfall again, and I had put on something nice to surprise him. As I skipped across Fenrir, the grandmother wolf stopped me where she gathered a basket of blooms. Calliach squeezed my arm in that tender and loving way only grandmothers knew how to do. "You make a wonderful mother wolf."

I smiled. "Thank you, though like I've told Wolfgang, I don't think motherhood is for me."

Calliach, in her wisdom and wolfish age, gifted me a wrinkled grin. "Fertility and breeding aren't all about making babies and sex. They're the essence of cultivating life, and that is done in ways that go far beyond wombs and bodily sensations. Many of us are mother wolves, and many of us have no pups, nor desire for them." She led me through a patch of clover as I listened intently to her storyteller's voice. "But we mother by leading, by being strong, and by cultivating our desires and passions. Being a mother is doing the hard thing for your family, making and acting on the decisions that gut you but have to be made. And it is our hope as lunas that we inspire others to do the same. When that catches on and those seeds are watered and tended to, they bloom for others as well." She let me go and spun, twirling her long white dress. She was a goddess if I'd ever seen one. A silver wolf, mother wolf, Mother Earth. "That is fertility within a luna. That's the heart of what we celebrate with spring. And you, Blythe, are certainly a mother wolf, if you want to be one."

True joy bloomed inside my soul. Being Death, I'd never considered mothering and life-giving, but she was right, and I did want to be a mother wolf in my own way. "That sounds perfect."

Wolf reclined on a patchwork quilt by the base of the waterfall. He made nature look small. He made the rushing water look insignificant next to his beauty. His amber eyes glowed more captivating than a show of fireflies. "That dress, that color pink…" he said by way of breathless greeting.

I giggled at how the man who'd torn apart monsters with his bare hands without breaking a sweat had become out of breath at the sight of me barefoot in a simple pink sundress. "Oh, you like it?" I teased, tugging a strap over my shoulder.

He grabbed my waist, and I yelped, laughing against his strength but never once afraid that he'd let me fall. Wolf would never let me fall.

Smelling my hair, he moved his lips to my ear. "Leave it on. The shade matches your blush, your nipples, your weeping pussy. Any man or mortal is blessed if he should get to make a woman come in a sundress. I want to fuck you like this, fuck you so good it's all you think about when you feel me spilling down your thighs, staining your little pink dress with my cum."

A needy whimper left my throat as my hips responded. "I may think of it," I managed to tease.

His sharp teeth flirted with my breasts as he bit the hem of my décolletage and yanked it down. "You're all I think of. This is all I think of. You're mine, little one, little moon."

"I'm so yours, Wolf," I admitted, wrapping my arms around his broad shoulders. A stature that swallowed the sun and chased the moon. My werewolf put the old legends of wolves to shame. He was the myths in pure, true form, and he was all mine. Wolfgang was folklore tied in a bow. His cock eased around my panties and pushed into me, kicking the breath from my chest. He moved with force, thrusting into me as soft splatters from the falls kissed my temples.

"I'm starving for you, Blythe. Let me eat you every day like this. I could swallow you whole and it wouldn't be enough," he ground out.

A scream left me as he buried himself to the hilt, hitting some deep place inside me. "Please," I begged. What was I begging for? Nothing and everything all at once, but my Wolf understood, and he gave it to me. He gave it to me over and over again, never faltering, never slowing. Each thrust was as ablaze as the last. His release spilled into me and filled me up. He'd made me a mother wolf and shown me how that had nothing to do with babies. And I'd love him for the rest of time and then after.

When we stilled, it was near dark, and I stood on shaking knees. "I'll be right back. I have to go find someone," I twirled my words about like Onyx taught me. It wasn't a lie; it was a truth twisted.

He nodded, sated for now. Slipping on my ballet flats, I followed the red path around the falls and into the meadow. I entered the berry patch, knowing Wolf could still smell me... would he still smell me after this?

I ran my fingertips over the bubbles of berries, and a bush shook, startling me. The wooden spirit giggled a sound worn ancient and newborn fresh. Smiling, I knelt next to them. "You're the willow spirit, aren't you?"

It nodded its round and twiggy head. "And you are Death and my friend."

With a smile I nodded. "Yes, I'm both of those things. So it looks like you got a new form. Why didn't you tell me?"

"I did. You just don't listen to the words not said." The Willow Spirit knocked on their rounded bark belly.

I laughed, tears pricking my eyes over what was about to happen. "I'm learning that to be true. But hey, I found your hiding spot." Oh, I was so happy I'd made friends with this tree. Without thinking, I pulled the little wooden spirit in for a hug, and they let me.

"Now it's your turn to hide, Blythe, and I will seek. Where will you go?"

"I think I have an idea… but it's a little of both hiding and seeking."

"Ah yes, all the best hiding spots are. I'll find you again soon. Remember to have fun with this game."

"I will." I smiled. "Look after my boys, please?"

The willow spirit smiled and backed away into a dark purple bush. They'd always be watching. I knew it to be true. Raven blocked out the sun as he circled me. I blew him a kiss. "That's your task now, too. Them, okay?"

He cawed a forlorn sound, but he'd obey, knowing he couldn't follow me where I was going. Standing, I walked down the aisles of berries until I reached the spot I remembered from my dream. "The end of all the riddles lead us here," I said softly, plucking a blackberry from a thorny branch. "Go ahead. I know you're watching."

Cold and darkness whistled with wind and swirled evil as a black circle opened in a huge, forbidding arch before me. I was afraid, but I had to keep the Halloween Boys safe. I had to keep my vision from happening.

Sometimes to get to heaven, you had to make a deal with the

devil. I took the berry between my teeth and bit down, letting the juice like sweet poison grind over my tongue. The deep and eerie voice of the devil radiated around me, chilling my bones and making me second-guess my decision as I stepped inside the portal.

"Welcome home, my bride."

A Secret

You're screaming and instead of comforting you I'm making you work. Less like an epilogue and more like a riddle, a baiting, a dark siren, but trust me, friends, it's oh so intriguing and dare I say *shocking and vital*… But you'll have to hunt like a wolf, stalk like a predator.

If you're a witch, you'll find it in the coven. If you're a pirate you'll have to find the board. If you're a black cat, you'll have to go to the place where the kat's black thorns collect names to send letters of all sorts.

Good luck.

THE DEVIL WAITS…

Acknowledgments

My loved ones, thank you for listening to my erratic voice messages rationalizing how wolf lore and The Halloween Boys melt together. For sitting around fires and exploring chaos magic, demon hierarchy, and begging for a Ghost + Onyx moment. (You're welcome)

My covens on Patreon and FB, for always hyping me up, making me laugh, and supporting this journey through the woods and over the mountain to grandmother's house. I'd offer you all a juicy apple if I could.

My Facebook Reader group, Kat Blackthorne and the Black Hearts Coven, who readily assisted with chapter title ideas that blew me away. Bevin Shea (fresh from the basket), Rachel McMahon (Hungry like a wolf), Chloe Montgomery (The stories we tell ourselves), Morgan Hill Nickles (Red or dead), Skylar Marie (moon song) and Ania Chrustek-Szaflik for suggesting Rammstein's "Du riechts so gut" for the playlist.

Artists, editors, storytellers for lending your magical spells.

The atrocious year that was 2016 that led me into the forest and comforted me with wolf howls, where tree spirits whispered the secrets of the mother wolf, thank you.

On to Halloween in Hell we go… follow me there, friends?

Chase Me

- Sign up for my newsletter to be the first to know about new book releases
- Join my patreon for first looks, early chapters of The Halloween Boys, secret projects, and more.
- Join me on #spicybooktok TikTok:
- See fan edits on Instagram:
- Follow for updates and quotes on Twitter:
- Follow me on Amazon for upcoming books:
- Join my reader coven on FB
- Please consider leaving a review on your favorite platform

Business or press inquires please email katblackthorneauthor@gmail.com

Also by Kat Blackthorne

The Halloween Boys

Ghost

Dragon

Wolf

Devil

Wicked Ecstasy

The other villains of Ash Grove

Come For A Spell

Familiar Taste

Lady Venom Takes a Mistress

Gothic lesbian romance

Hot Queens

Contemporary polyamory

Hotwife

Hot Life

Let it Snow Queen

Browse by Trope for more

at katblackthorne.com